Santa's
Mail-Order
Bride

SEQUEL TO VICTORIA, BRIDE OF KANSAS

E.E. BURKE

Cover Design by Erin Dameron-Hill
Train photography by Matthew Malkeiwicz
Interior formatting by Author E.M.S.

Published by E.E. Burke
ISBN: 978-0-9969822-2-1

Dedication

*This book is dedicated to my dear friend in Fort Scott,
"Miss Pat" Lyons.*

*Thank you for sharing your beautiful Twin Mansions
and your love for the past.*

Chapter One

December 7, 1892, Fort Scott, Kansas

"Every child deserves a Christmas present." Maggie O'Brien paced the length of her brother's general store with her fifteen-month-old nephew propped on her hip. The gleeful toddler tugged at loose strands of hair no longer in an artful arrangement. She tickled him to distract him. "Isn't that right, Paddy?"

The cherub laughed and said something that sounded like *Mama*.

"Yes, your Mama is busy now. Look at all these people buying presents. Wouldn't it be nice if some of these gifts could be sent to the orphans? Don't you agree, Victoria?"

Her sister-in-law finished wrapping a purchase in brown paper, smiling as she handed it to a customer, while Maggie's brother David waited on a gentleman purchasing a hobbyhorse.

"I do agree," Victoria answered, after the customer walked away. "Every child deserves to be shown love."

Hugging Patrick to her, Maggie sidestepped a distracted couple accompanied by three children. The youngest, a boy, stopped to examine a sack of marbles, while two older girls wandered over to a display featuring paper dolls with crepe paper clothing, a gift that would appeal to her niece Fannie. Customers were packed into O'Brien's today, taking advantage of the unexpected sunshine to do some Christmas shopping.

Not every child had someone who loved them purchasing hobbyhorses, marbles and dolls, and Maggie's heart ached for those orphaned children. Worse, homeless children in Kansas were put to work on poor farms or languished at dingy facilities crowded with impoverished adults.

This year, Maggie had come home on a mission: to collect gifts for orphaned children in the area and distribute them by Christmas Eve. How she'd accomplish this, she wasn't sure. She had a list of fifty names. Collecting that many gifts in roughly three weeks boggled the mind, but she was determined to show these children they were not forgotten.

David looked over the next customer's shoulder. "It's not us you need to convince, Maggie."

"I know. You're being very generous."

Not surprisingly, her brother had agreed to aid her. They both had a soft spot for orphans, having lost their parents at an early age. They'd been fortunate to be taken in, but David had been forced to drop out of school at age twelve to go to work so he could support them.

Homeless children also needed schooling as well as to have their basic needs met. Sadly, she didn't have the wealth or the influence to make that happen anytime soon. She could, however, provide Christmas presents—if she could find enough backers.

Maggie walked over to the large glass window overlooking the street. Wagons and buggies lined the hitching post in front of O'Brien's. Mr. Sumner's Five Cent Store also appeared busy, as usual. The two stores, directly across from each other, engaged in heated competition. David had nearly been forced to close his doors two years ago, until he'd made changes to the store. The progressive merchant across the street had few scruples when it came to competition. He would undoubtedly come up with some new way to harass her brother.

She continued walking with Patrick to keep him entertained, pausing at a table with a display of mechanical toys. When Patrick reached for a wind-up train, she did a quick twirl on her heel and headed for safe territory. How his parents kept him from turning the store upside down was beyond her. She didn't dare put him on his feet. Forget bull in a china shop, he was a frolicking calf.

"Is this Patrick, or do my eyes deceive me?" One of the customers, Mrs. Robinson, waylaid them. The stately matron had more lines in her face than last year, and her steps seemed slower. There was nothing slow about her mind. Her eyes snapped with intelligence and curiosity. "Miss O'Brien, it's good to see you again. You're home for good, or just for Christmas?"

"Only through Christmas, and then it's back to the schoolroom."

"How do you like Kansas City? I hear that cow town will soon be more populous than Fort Scott, though I can hardly believe it."

"Oh, that's a fact, what with all the railroads and the stockyards." Maggie loved the bustle and excitement of the growing city, but she missed home far more than she'd thought she would. She'd been gone two years, off teaching, which was what she'd always wanted to do. She would be forever grateful to her older brother, who had scrimped and saved to send her to a teacher's college. He'd sacrificed so much for her. She would never let him down.

Mrs. Robinson patted Patrick's back as he bounced on Maggie's hip. "You're getting to be a big boy."

"Yes, indeed." Maggie lifted her nephew's compact weight higher and smiled at him. "How big is Paddy?"

With a huge grin, he lifted his arms in the air and stretched them out as far as he could.

"*Sooo* big," Maggie dragged out the first word, to the delight of her nephew.

Patrick giggled and patted her cheek. She'd earned an *A* with the correct response. *So big* had become his favorite game, next to pulling the cat's tail.

"What a sweet-tempered child," Mrs. Robinson cooed. "And he looks just like his father."

"That he does." Maggie had rather hoped her brother's child would have his mother's striking aqua eyes and golden hair. Not surprisingly, Paddy had inherited the black O'Brien eyes and hair, as had his father and his aunt and his half-sister Fannie. But, oh, he was a beautiful boy, healthy and happy, just as every child should be.

Mrs. Robinson gave Patrick another fond pat. The wealthy matron served on the board of St. Andrew's Episcopal, the oldest church in town, and had her finger in every pie when it came to local charities. She would be a perfect person to ask for help.

"Have you ever seen a *poor farm*?"

The widow appeared puzzled by Maggie's question. "No, can't say that I have."

"It's a sad place, I can tell you." Maggie couldn't get the images out of her mind. *Poor farm* was an appropriate moniker for those awful places. "They work the children like slaves, and still there's barely enough to feed and clothe them. I have a list of fifty orphans just from this area alone that won't have a Christmas if we don't do something about it. I'm collecting gifts for them. David and Victoria have been very generous, but their contributions won't be enough. Could you suggest others who might help? Churches, perhaps?

The elderly lady's face folded into a sad smile. "That's very kind of you, my dear, but I wouldn't count on the churches for more than what they've already committed to doing. They all have collections this time of year to help needy families. You'll have to look elsewhere, I'm afraid."

Maggie's spirits dipped. She thought it would be easier to gain support, especially around Christmastime, but this was the message she'd heard from several other people.

"You say your brother is donating goods?" the older woman asked.

"Yes, clothes and toys."

"What about asking that nice gentleman across the street for donations? Mr. Sumner ought to be willing to match his competitor." Mrs. Robinson's eyes twinkled. "If you make a personal request."

Soliciting donations from the owner of the second largest store in Fort Scott would be a good suggestion, if it didn't require talking to him. Not to mention, Gordon Sumner would be unlikely to help the sister of his chief competitor, even if she made her plea *personally*.

Maggie shifted Patrick to her other hip, and lowered her voice so others in the store couldn't hear her. "I doubt Mr. Sumner would be open to any request I'd make. He and David don't get along."

"My dear, if you're determined to have those gifts, you may have to mend a few fences." Mrs. Robinson kissed Paddy's cheek and then took her leave.

"She's right, you know," came a soft voice from behind.

Maggie turned to meet her sister-in-law's knowing

gaze. Victoria didn't have a mean bone in her body, not even one reserved for her husband's archrival. "Not you, too."

"Contrary to what you and David seem to think, Mr. Sumner doesn't have fangs and claws. He's very civil, and I suspect he would be happy to help you."

"You're the soul of kindness, Victoria. The man could be a wolf in disguise and you'd invite him to dinner."

Maggie would never admit she'd taken notice of the handsome Mr. Sumner. What woman wouldn't? But the eligible Easterner flirted with every young lady in town. He wouldn't be interested in her in particular even if she wanted him to be, which she didn't, not even if he did have lovely auburn hair and the bluest eyes she'd ever seen.

Victoria glanced over at her husband, who'd started frowning the moment Sumner's name was mentioned. "We needn't extend a dinner invitation. All you're asking for is a donation." She reached out for Patrick. "Here, I'll take him. It's time for his lunch and a nap."

Patrick began to fuss the moment he heard the word *nap*.

Victoria rubbed his back soothingly. "Thank you for watching him, Maggie."

"I loved every minute," Maggie pressed a kiss on the toddler's head. He smelled warm and sweet, just like a baby should smell. She adored her nephew and her eight-year-old niece and missed being around them.

She had lived with her brother and looked after Fannie for a troubled two years after David's first wife had abandoned them. He'd been miserable until Victoria came along.

Maggie took no small amount of pride in her matchmaking efforts. Thanks to her, David had found his true love. She longed to discover that same rare connection. Growing up, she had always dreamed of finding her soul's mate, but at the advanced age of twenty-four, she had yet to meet a man who made her heart race.

"I'll walk over to the school and meet Fannie," she told Victoria. "There's a Christmas tree exhibit at Convention Hall I'd like to show her."

"She'd love that, I'm sure." Victoria stroked her son's silky hair as he laid his head on her shoulder. "And do consider Mrs. Robinson's suggestion. You'll need all the help you can muster if you're determined to collect fifty gifts by Christmas."

Maggie sighed with resignation. She had avoided charming Mr. Sumner because her loyalty would always be to her family, and heaven forbid she might actually like the man. But her sister-in-law was right. Nothing should get in the way of collecting those gifts, not even her reluctance to do business with a dapper carnivore.

She straightened her shoulders. "I'll pay Mr. Sumner a visit this afternoon after the stores have closed for business."

Chapter Two

G ordon Sumner slammed the account book shut. Another round of calculations wouldn't improve the numbers. He glared at a stack of letters on the desk next to the lamp, then jerked open a drawer, crammed the unopened envelopes inside and shut it. Why bother reading them? He knew Sikes had passed the point of impatience six months ago. Sales had better be stellar this Christmas, or he was in big trouble.

He grasped the gold fob and drew his watch from a vest pocket. Six o'clock. Time to lock up. For the month of December, he'd kept the store open an hour later than usual, in hopes of snagging his competitor's customers. O'Brien's always closed at five sharp. Had the other store folded last year as anticipated, his problems would have been solved. Somehow, the stubborn Irishman hung on. He'd even expanded and improved the interior, and his efforts had paid off. By all signs, O'Brien's was doing well.

Sum swore. He would win this battle. This time he wouldn't fail.

Standing, he pocketed the watch and left his office.

He'd go downstairs, collect the day's proceeds from the till and tell the clerk she could go home, if she hadn't left already.

When he first opened his Five Cent Store, he anticipated needing only a single clerk to manage the cash register. Unlike the old fashioned shebang, his goods were displayed in clear view and marked with prices, eliminating the necessity of clerks' collecting items on a customer's list. He hired Anna Smith and then discovered having pretty women around helped his business, so he hired a few more like her, mostly as window dressing.

Even with an improvement in sales, he couldn't afford window dressing. Over the past year, he'd let go of all but one clerk. After the Christmas rush, he would, regrettably, have to do without Miss Smith. He hated to dismiss the hardworking young woman, knowing the girl was her family's only source of income since her father had been killed in a mining accident and her mother had fallen ill. After his debts were cleared, he would rehire Miss Smith.

The overhead lights burned brightly, but the store appeared to be empty, except for a woman standing in front the Christmas display. That wasn't his clerk. However, he would recognize her anywhere, even from the back—the Irishman's sister.

Sum's mood improved. He'd wanted to get to know the black-haired beauty ever since meeting her on his first day in town, but she'd avoided him like he carried a plague. Then she had moved away. She must've come home for Christmas. That didn't explain what had brought her into his store. Why speculate when he could ask?

"Miss O'Brien. May I help you?"

She turned, her brown cloak swirling around a green plaid skirt. The woodsy colors complemented her dark hair and gypsy eyes. "Ah, Mr. Sumner, good evening. I thought the store might be closed, but your lights were on."

"We've extended our hours this season. Did Miss Smith let you in?"

"Your clerk said to tell you she had to leave to pick up some medicine for her mother. She...she said it was all right if I looked around while I waited."

His lovely visitor flushed a becoming shade of pink and clutched a small handbag to her chest. Had the Irish lass ever shown a smidgeon of interest, he might've interpreted her reaction as a virginal woman's response to a man who fired her blood. He didn't presume that to be the case with Miss O'Brien. Still, he couldn't help being pleased she'd sought him out for some purpose.

"You're welcome in my store anytime." He reached up to straighten his tie before remembering he'd pulled the bow loose and unbuttoned his collar, deciding he might as well be comfortable as he reviewed the books—a process that made every item he wore feel as if it pinched. Not only that, he'd left his coat upstairs. Greeting a lady wearing a wrinkled shirt and waistcoat wasn't how one made a good impression.

Impressing Miss O'Brien shouldn't be high on his list of priorities. She was his adversary's sister, therefore, not to be trusted. If he had the sense of a clam, he'd close his shell.

Clams weren't known for their intelligence.

She made a brief assessment of the store before regarding him quizzically. "You've invested a great deal into furnishings. Where did you find the etched globes and maple display cases?"

A laugh bubbled up his throat. "You came in here to talk about my furnishings?"

"No..." She fussed with the drawstrings on her bag, twisting them around her fingers, looking everywhere but at him. "I came over here to ask you for money."

His ego took a hard fall. "Money?"

"Or goods, either would do." The tip of her tongue sneaked out and moistened her lips.

He had the most insane thought that if she offered a kiss in exchange, he would grant her wishes. However, he couldn't imagine why she'd ask him for money, unless her brother was in financial straits.

Sum arranged his face in a look of concern to hide a very uncharitable emotion. "May I take your cloak? We could sit down and have a cup of coffee while we discuss your, um, needs."

Her blush deepened to crimson. "That's not necessary. It's not my needs I'm concerned with at the moment, or yours. The gifts are for the orphans."

"The orphans?" Not what he'd expected her to say, nor was it a fascinating topic. Given the choice, he'd rather talk about her. "You could spare a few minutes, surely? After all, you've made a rather curious request, and should I grant it, I'd like to know more."

Unease flickered across her face. She had no desire to linger, and if his guess was right, she loathed the very idea of seeking him out.

His self-confidence was taking a beating.

"Very well. I'll stay for a short visit." She turned, allowing him to take her wrap.

As he drew the cloak off her shoulders, an intriguing scent teased his nose. Peppermint. How delightful...she smelled of candy. His mouth watered.

With no small effort, he dragged his mind away from inappropriate longings. Sweet or not, she didn't belong to him. Therefore, he had no business kissing the back of her neck, no matter how good she smelled.

Sum draped the cloak over his arm. He gestured in the direction of the back counter, where stools were set up for shoppers who wished to tarry and indulge in pastries or a sandwich. "All the baked goods have been purchased, or I would offer you something to eat."

"Thank you, I'm not hungry."

"Coffee or tea? I could make either.

"No, thank you. I'm not thirsty."

Not easy to please, apparently. But what beautiful woman was? He could be smitten if she sent him one tiny signal that she shared this insane attraction.

He waited until she sat down before he slipped onto a stool next to her, and his knee brushed against her skirt.

She twisted to one side to open space between them. Modesty. Or she might fear he would pounce. He found her skittishness charming.

"Just who are these orphans? They must be important to have compelled you to enter my lair...I mean, store."

Her lips didn't so much as twitch.

He adopted a droll tone. "Rumor has it, you have a sense of humor."

"I do, when something's funny."

He smoothed his mustache to wipe away a smile. She probably wouldn't appreciate him saying he found her amusing, as well as alluring.

Her gaze became very direct. Her dark eyes were nearly black, and yet her skin glowed with pale opalescence. Exquisite. "I won't waste any more of your time."

"You're not wasting my time—"

"Have you ever been to a poor farm, Mr. Sumner?"

She was about to play on his heartstrings with a sad tale. Thus far this season, he'd heard no less than a dozen pathetic stories and had spared all the good will he could afford. She should've shown up earlier. But he would listen to her plea, especially if it meant she would stay longer.

"No, I haven't been to a poor farm, if by that you

mean one of those places they put orphans to work. I presume you have?"

Her expression grew somber. "Yes. Fortunately, I never had to live on one. After our parents died, my brother and I moved in with an elderly shopkeeper and his wife. I suspect we would've ended up on a poor farm had David not gone to work to support us."

Sum frowned at the surprising revelation. He'd heard her brother had reopened his parents' business, but he hadn't known the couple died early. "How old were you when they passed away?"

"They were killed in a fire when I was four and David was ten." She looked down at her lap, fiddling with the fringe along the bottom of her purse.

Sum had a burning desire to know more about her past, but he wouldn't probe if it made her uncomfortable. She appeared achingly young and vulnerable, and he had a sudden urge to put his arms around her. He was sure that gesture wouldn't be welcomed. "That explains why you have a heart for orphans."

She looked up with surprise. "I hope you share my concern, Mr. Sumner. I've committed to providing gifts for fifty orphaned children. That's why I'm asking for your contribution."

Contrary to what she might've heard, he did have a heart. She might have better luck than most with breaking it, if he wasn't careful. "Of course I share your concern. Only a hardhearted brute wouldn't."

Miss O'Brien rewarded him with a warm smile. "I'm relieved to hear you are a man of compassion. Victoria felt sure you would help."

Another surprise. He hadn't imagined the wealthy Boston Brahmin-turned-shopkeeper's wife had a soft spot in her heart for him. Two years ago, he'd flirted with her when she'd ventured over to his store, and then tweaked O'Brien's nose when he'd charged in to claim her. "How nice to know Mrs. O'Brien speaks well of me."

"Oh, I wouldn't go that far. My sister-in-law only said she expected you to match my brother's contribution."

Clever girl. She'd thrown down a gauntlet, O'Brien's generosity.

Sum wouldn't be bested. "How much do you need?"

"My brother is donating generously. He's providing gifts for five children. Would you be willing to do the same?"

He would, except he had no excess inventory. He couldn't afford to give away goods, and he had no extra cash on hand. Being woefully behind on repaying his debts, he didn't dare give freely.

"Mr. Sumner? Can I count on you for a contribution?"

He forced a smile, inwardly chiding himself for walking into an ambush. She'd used unfair tactics to distract him, her lovely face and form, and her delicious scent. "You'll need more than clothes and gifts for ten children."

"Yes, we need gifts for fifty. Could you manage more than five? I have a list." She eagerly dug into her purse.

He couldn't manage two. But…if he could figure out a way to get other people to pitch in to meet her quota, then that would solve her problem and make him look like a hero.

Sliding off the stool, he began to pace. Thinking was easier when he moved. "There's not much time left."

"I know, I should've started earlier," she bemoaned.

"Don't lose hope. We'll come up with something."

"We?" She withdrew her hand from her purse. "I haven't formed a committee, nor do I recall asking you to be on one."

"Good. Committees take too long. If your volunteers are as difficult as those fools in charge of the Christmas parade, you'll never get anything done."

He came to an abrupt halt as his mind latched onto an idea. Oh, it was a good one. Not only would she gain the necessary contributions, but he would garner additional publicity, even more than what he'd hoped for in agreeing to don a costume and play the part of old St. Nick.

"The parade," he murmured. "Yes. That would be perfect."

"Parade? Perfect?" She shook her head. "I'm sorry, I'm not following."

"This year, I'm sponsoring Santa's sleigh and dressing the part. What if, instead of giving gifts, Santa Claus requests contributions to his list, all of which will be delivered to the orphans by Christmas Eve."

Miss O'Brien's lovely lips parted and her eyes widened with surprise. "Oh! Oh, Mr. Sumner, that's brilliant!" She clapped her hands together like a delighted child, and then leapt off the stool and threw her arms around his neck. "How can I ever thank you?"

Oh, he could come up with several suggestions.

He leaned down to hug her and ended up crushing her soft breasts against his chest. Every muscle in his body tensed, as desire buried him in an avalanche. Throwing caution to the wind, he picked her up and twirled her around. Before he released her, he stole a quick kiss.

"We'll get your orphans gifts, Miss O'Brien. I promise you."

Her dazed expression remained, as her cheeks bloomed with color and her hands floated up to her mouth. At least she didn't slap him.

His heart pumped liquid fire through his veins, the brief touch only whetting his appetite for more. He

15

vowed to get a longer, deeper kiss before Miss O'Brien waltzed out of his life again, and he knew just how he would engineer it.

"You...you..." she sputtered.

"Kissed you? Yes. That's what a man does with his wife."

She scurried backwards, the high color draining from her face. "What are you talking about? I'm not your wife."

"Not mine, Santa's. You, my dear, will be Mrs. Claus."

Chapter Three

Three days later, Mr. Sumner showed up to escort Maggie to a meeting of the Christmas Parade committee, where they would present his idea. Not the part about Mrs. Claus. The flirtatious rascal would never convince her to be his temporary wife, pretend or otherwise. The whole town would think she'd set her cap for him.

The day had dawned sparkling bright—the kind of winter morning when the sun lights up a clear blue sky and temperatures drop down low enough to freeze smiles into place. Just walking the short distance to the offices of the *Fort Scott Monitor and Tribune* turned her hands and feet into blocks of ice.

Mr. Sumner appeared unfazed by the cold and talked the entire way.

Maggie hadn't realized he could be so chatty, although it ended up being a good thing because she was nervous and it spared her from having to converse much. "Are you sure they'll approve your recommendation?" she asked as they neared the brick building at the corner of Wall Street.

"If we're in agreement, I don't see why not."

Maggie hesitated, and not for the first time. David hadn't liked the idea of his competitor's personal involvement in her project, but he'd gone along with it for her sake. She couldn't let him down by doing anything that would embarrass him, such as posing as Mr. Sumner's parade wife. "I'm agreeable to your Santa collecting gifts," she clarified.

When they reached the newspaper offices, Mr. Sumner indicated a bench in the front hallway. Taking her cloak, he hung it on a nearby hall tree and then sat next to her.

"We're to wait here until we're summoned."

Maggie couldn't resist returning his impudent smile. The parade committee included Fort Scott's most influential citizens and some of the members acted like royalty.

Mr. Sumner squeezed in next to her on the bench, which had armrests carved into the shape of lion's claws. Somehow this seemed fitting, given her companion's predatory nature. After last night, she would be on guard for any unexpected attacks, such as that kiss he'd given her. To her mortal shame, she couldn't stop thinking about it. What had possessed him? Or did he go about kissing every lady he met?

She removed her gloves and flexed her fingers. "My hands are still frozen. It's hard to believe it can be so bitterly cold when the sun is shining."

"Appearances can be deceiving," he noted.

Indeed. Gordon Sumner appeared to be a gentleman. But gentlemen didn't kiss ladies without permission.

As a distraction, Maggie arranged folds in the sumptuous velvet skirt. She'd put on her most festive outfit, with a pine green jacket trimmed in red braid, and a matching figured bonnet. Mr. Sumner had complimented her so effusively she'd gotten embarrassed. Resisting the charmer would be easier if he weren't so amusing, not to mention handsome as sin.

He'd unbuttoned his double-breasted overcoat to reveal a fashionable gray suit with a contrasting waistcoat. The points of his starched white collar were neatly turned down, and he wore a colorful four-in-hand tie. *Looking savage*, as David would say, to impress the committee, no doubt about it. Then again, she couldn't recall a time Mr. Sumner didn't look impressive.

Her gaze drifted upward to his lips, framed by a cinnamon-colored mustache. Their kiss had lasted no more than an instant, yet in that moment something inside her shifted, and she had the strangest impression her life had changed direction, like a train switching tracks. Ridiculous, because nothing had changed, the kiss hadn't meant anything, even if it had made her lips tingle. That must've been on account of his mustache. She hadn't expected it to be so soft. And the tickle surprised her.

Drat, the tingling had started up again.

He smiled.

She met an admiring blue gaze and blushed. He'd caught her staring.

Flustered, she blurted the first thing that came to mind "Are you cold?" She formed a core with her hands and blew into it. "I should've brought thicker gloves."

"Give me your hands," he commanded.

Instead of waiting to see if she would comply, he reached over and took what he wanted, sandwiching her chilled fingers between his palms, creating a gentle friction. After a moment, delicious warmth suffused her hands. The heat crept up her arms and spread throughout her entire body.

"Thank you. Much better now." She tried to remove her hands. He wouldn't let go.

"You're still cold."

That wasn't why she was shivering.

"I'm not cold. Not anymore."

One of the men who worked for the newspaper strode down the hallway. He glanced over, eyeing them with a quizzical expression. Alarmed, she tugged her hands free and then flattened them on the seat. Whatever Mr. Sumner was up to, she wanted no part of it.

In fact, he'd surprised her when he'd suggested the gift collection idea and then offered to help her implement it. What could he possibly gain, save getting more coverage in the newspaper? "Why are you doing this?" she whispered.

He rested his hand over hers. "Warming you up?"

His touch did more than warm her; it sent alarming quivers across her skin and made her heart jump. The dratted man put her off balance. Somehow, she had to find her way back to equilibrium. First, she had better acknowledge reality. He wasn't her beau, and she would never be his bride, pretend or otherwise.

She removed her hand from beneath his and curled her fingers in her lap. "What I mean is, why are you helping me? Not out of sympathy for the children."

"You don't think I'm sympathetic?" His tone implied she'd wounded him, though it was difficult to tell if he was teasing or serious.

"I only wondered if you might see this as an opportunity to polish your reputation."

"So you believe me to be mercenary, as well as heartless." This time there was no mistaking his reaction. He looked puzzled, even a little hurt.

Her conscience took her to task. "Forgive me if I misread your intentions." That wasn't good enough. She had insulted him. "You've been very kind, and I do appreciate your help."

"My pleasure."

He spoke in a smooth baritone, low and resonant, like

the purr of a very large cat. He hadn't curled up beside her, but he sat very close...close enough to make her heart beat faster, and her breathing quicken.

Footsteps sounded on the hardwood floors. Mr. Marble, the newspaper editor, approached. He had a pencil tucked behind his ear. "Mr. Sumner, Miss O'Brien. The committee is ready to discuss your proposal."

"Excellent." Her companion stood and offered his assistance. Maggie allowed him to tuck her hand into the crook of his arm because that was the polite thing to do. Had she been able to avoid touching him, she would have. The effect was far too stimulating.

They entered a large, dim room, made darker because of the wood paneling on the walls. Heavy curtains had been drawn over the windows to keep out the cold. Light from a chandelier illuminated an oval table and twelve committee members sitting around it.

The gentlemen stood as she entered. Feeling ridiculously shy, she clung to Mr. Sumner's arm. She knew every person sitting at that table, had known most of them all of her life, but that didn't make her any less nervous. David was the one who had business dealings with grownups. She was more comfortable in front of a roomful of children.

"Good morning, ladies and gentleman." Mr. Sumner sounded confident and at ease, as if he presented in front of important people all the time.

Mr. O'Connor, who insisted everyone call him *Buck*, gestured to two chairs. "Mr. Sumner, Miss O'Brien, please sit down."

The elder businessman cut an intimidating figure at well over six feet, with rugged features, flowing white hair and sharp gray eyes. His wife, seated next to him, had rich brown hair lightly marked with gray and an ageless kind of beauty. Although petite, she had an authoritative air, which made her nearly as intimidating as her husband.

Mr. Sumner pulled out a chair. He laid his hand on Maggie's shoulder in a brief, comforting touch, before taking the seat next to her.

Mrs. O'Connor sent her an encouraging smile. "Good to see you back in town, Miss O'Brien. How long will you remain in town?"

Before Maggie could respond, an older woman with a pointed stare interrupted. "We understand you wish to *collect* gifts this year instead of giving them away."

The disdainful tone sent Maggie's hackles up. Oh, she had seen that one in the store a few times, although the rich lady didn't purchase readymade items. Mrs. Mueller ordered her dresses from Eastern designers, along with fashionable hats, including the one she had on, which featured stuffed birds pasted to the side. She and her hat were equally gruesome.

"That's right, Mrs. Mueller, we wish to collect gifts for a charitable purpose." Mr. Sumner spoke before Maggie could make her tongue move. His wry smile made her wonder whether he shared similar feelings about the woman and her hat.

He'd remarked earlier that they might meet resistance from the town's wealthiest patron, who'd come up with the idea for the Christmas parade and considered it her personal project. Even her nickname, Old Ironsides, implied trouble.

"Miss O'Brien, would you like to explain our cause?" With that, Mr. Sumner gave her the floor.

"Yes, of course." She dug into her bag and retrieved the list. "I have the names of fifty orphans across Bourbon and Linn counties who won't receive gifts for Christmas unless we provide them. Most live on poor farms. Have any of you ever been to a poor farm?"

Mrs. Mueller's nostrils flared like she smelled

something offensive. "No, I'm not in the habit of sticking my nose into other peoples' business."

Only telling them what to do.

With effort, Maggie put on a pleasant face. "But mankind *is* our business, is that not what Mr. Dickens wrote in his fine tale? These children's lives are miserable. They work like slaves, they're barely fed and clothed, and provided with no education. It breaks my heart."

Her voice wavered with emotion. She longed to improve the plight of orphaned children in Kansas, and this small, yet meaningful step could draw attention to the problem. "Giving them Christmas presents isn't nearly enough, but it's a start."

The matron glanced around at the somber expressions, and then cleared her throat. "That does sound like a very serious problem, but it's not something we can solve with a parade. Our Santa is supposed to bring gifts, not take them. If he doesn't distribute presents, the local children will be disappointed."

Charlie Goodlander leaned back in his chair, his substantial weight making it creak. He twirled one end of a walrus mustache, looking thoughtful. "Of course we love our traditions, but what Mr. Sumner and Miss O'Brien are suggesting is for a good cause."

Maggie's spirits lifted. The outspoken president of the Citizens' National Bank, one of the town's original settlers, was exactly the kind of person they needed behind this project.

"The idea is worth considering," he went on. "We might even be able to establish an orphanage right here in Fort Scott, if we can raise money every year during the parade—"

"There are *many* good causes, Mr. Goodlander," Old Ironsides insisted. "If we allowed every one of them to pre-empt our event, it would be a disaster. The people of

Fort Scott love the Christmas parade and Santa arriving to bless the children. It's the most popular attraction of the year. I vote we keep things the way they've always been."

The old biddy didn't care about blessing anyone. She only wanted to exert control, as if her vote was the only one that counted. Perhaps it was, considering how quiet everyone became.

Mrs. O'Connor broke the silence. "We're not voting yet, Mabel. Our rules call for discussion first."

God bless Mrs. O'Connor. She'd put Old Ironsides and her dead birds in their place.

The committee commenced to *discuss*, which ended up being more of an argument. The O'Connors and Mr. Goodlander supported the proposal, two other members supported Mrs. Mueller, and the rest remained undecided.

Mr. Sumner leaned her way. "This is ridiculous," he whispered.

He scooted his chair back and stood, which got everyone's attention. "Honorable ladies and gentlemen, consider how it might look if you don't support this effort. Should Miss O'Brien's request be rebuffed, the leaders of the community will look like Scrooges."

Mrs. Mueller's florid face turned a deeper shade of red. "Just how do you suppose that? Santa arriving with gifts reflects the soul of generosity. The children in Fort Scott, including those from needy families, should be our first concern. We won't look miserly—unless you fail to provide the donations you promised."

Mr. Sumner sat down. Being close, Maggie could see the hard set of his jaw.

Old Ironsides narrowed her eyes as if spotting a weakness she could exploit. "Mr. Sumner, you did agree to sponsor Santa's sleigh this year. That sponsorship includes providing toys and other items to be given away. Or are you saying you don't have them."

"We'll have what we need," he stated with uncustomary brevity.

Maggie's stomach somersaulted. Now it was clear why he'd suggested a Santa gift collection. He'd promised gifts for the parade and wasn't in a position to make another generous contribution, and it was his way of making up for the deficit. But now, his plan might backfire. For certain, he wouldn't benefit from being at odds with these influential people. He really was a kind man, but he didn't have to shoulder this responsibility.

She dug in her bag for a peppermint to calm her queasiness. The fragrant scent wafted upwards. Apparently, Mr. Sumner could smell it because he'd turned to look at her, wearing an apologetic smile.

"Do you have any ideas for how we might keep our tradition, and still be able to collect gifts for the orphans?" he asked.

"She doesn't have an idea. Let's vote," Mrs. Mueller demanded.

Maggie rolled the candy between her thumb and forefinger. "Actually, I do have an idea." She stood and held up the candy. "This is what I propose."

"Peppermints?" Old Ironsides huffed.

Mr. Goodlander leaned forward. "I'll have one, thank you."

Maggie retrieved another candy and passed it to the bank president. She prayed her brother would support her, and made a silent promise to find a way to repay him.

"Every year, Santa gives gifts, but there are never enough to go around to all the children. What if this year Santa arrives with candy instead? If Mr. Sumner and my brother pool their resources, we can provide an ample amount of candy to go around. And we can post Santa's list and ask people to bring gifts for the orphans."

"Santa doesn't collect gifts," Mrs. Mueller insisted.

Mr. Sumner splayed his hands on the gleaming table surface, looking as if he'd like to leap across and throttle the wretched woman. "Then have a *Mrs. Claus* do it."

Maggie shot him an alarmed look, which he didn't catch and kept talking.

"Mrs. Claus can post a list of gifts she needs for the orphaned children. You, Mr. Marble, can write a column about it, include the items, and ask people to bring them the day of the parade. Mrs. Claus will collect them at my store and at O'Brien's."

Maggie released a slow breath. At least he hadn't committed *her* to playing the role.

"That's a wonderful idea," Mrs. O'Connor declared. She snatched up her husband's gavel and smacked it on the table. "Let's vote and call it done."

"We've never had a Mrs. Claus," blustered the naysayer.

"There's always a first time." Mr. O'Connor retrieved his gavel. "And I think it adds a nice touch. It'll appeal to the women, seeing Mrs. Claus riding beside her husband and helping him pass out candy, and gathering the gifts together. I vote for it, too."

He cradled the gavel and peered around the table with a challenging look.

"Count me in." Mr. Goodlander, who appeared amused by the gavel-wielding duo, lifted a forefinger. The rest of the committee quickly voiced their agreement, all but Mrs. Mueller.

"Who will play the part of Mrs. Claus?" she challenged. "I certainly won't."

Maggie couldn't imagine anyone asking her. She had the sourest personality. Victoria might. No. David would have a fit.

"Miss O'Brien, of course." Mr. O'Connor smacked his gavel, making Maggie jump. "After all, it's her project, and her brother is helping supply candy. Just makes sense."

"The two of us together..." Mr. Sumner turned to her, his cerulean gaze questioning. "What do you say, Miss O'Brien?"

He made it sound as if she had a choice. Of course she didn't, unless she wanted another round of arguments, which might end up burying the entire proposal. She'd backed herself into this corner, and had committed her brother, too. Not only that, if she refused, she would embarrass Mr. Sumner. She couldn't do that. Not after all he'd done for her.

Knowing full well she'd regret it, Maggie nevertheless gave in with gracious smile. "Yes, I'd be delighted to play the part of Mrs. Claus."

Chapter Four

I t took Sum two days to dislodge Miss O'Brien from her brother's store so they could go to a seamstress and have costumes fitted for the parade. A winter storm had moved in and dumped a foot of snow on the ground—that was her excuse anyway.

"Stay close to me so you don't become chilled." He wrapped his arm around her waist to steady her on the snow-packed sidewalks as they mushed along for six blocks.

"I'm not cold."

So she said, but she didn't pull away. At least she'd bundled up in a hooded cloak and scarf, with thicker gloves and sturdier boots, which looked warmer than the button-up shoes she'd worn the day of the meeting. Still, he didn't want her to get chilled and come down ill.

"We could hop aboard a street car." The one lumbering past had passengers in every seat and overflowing the aisles. Two men standing on the steps clung to outside rails.

Miss O'Brien shook her head. "Too crowded. We'll get there faster if we walk briskly."

Her legs were much shorter than his, but he had to press his pace to keep up with her. When they reached their destination, he checked his timepiece. "Your brisk walking set a new record. We made it in less than ten minutes."

"Does it normally take you longer?" She regarded him with a look that said he must be a lazy fellow if he couldn't make the distance within that time.

They sought warmth inside the cozy shop. The tailor and his wife who ran the business together appeared to be doing well, if the multiple racks of clothing in various stages of completion were any indication.

After Sum explained what they wanted, Mrs. Bowman shooed them into separate dressing rooms. The buxom brunette had years and energy to spare, compared to her stooped, elderly husband. Rumor had it, the old tailor was a single widower for nigh on twenty years, and then one day, a young woman showed up in his shop. He'd introduced her as his new bride, ordered from back east.

Despite being in the merchandising business, Sum considered the practice of ordering a wife ludicrous. Brides and grooms routinely misrepresented themselves, and someone was bound to be disappointed. He suspected Mrs. Bowman hadn't gotten the virile husband she'd expected, but she put on a good show of being happy with her lot in life.

Mr. Bowman muttered under his breath as he took Sum's measurements. He tottered off to the back room, still muttering. Assuming the fitting was done, Sum ducked back into the shop, hearing cheery conversation.

The two women chatted about the inclement weather, a favorite topic of late, as the tailor's wife measured her customer's trim waist. Sum considered offering his assistance, but the seamstress stood up and put away her measuring tape. Maybe another time.

Sum propped his arm on the doorframe, admiring Miss O'Brien's unguarded profile. No falsely represented female here, she was the real thing: beautiful, kind, gracious, and, as an added bonus, educated—a schoolteacher, no less.

He could think of no reason why he shouldn't pursue her, save his financial uncertainty, which would be resolved after Christmas with any luck. He wasn't getting any younger. Having a wife would grant him more respectability—and admiration, should his wife happen to be the lovely and gifted Miss O'Brien. Granted, she was his competitor's sister, but he would find a way to manage the consequences. If he had let thorny moral dilemmas stop him when he was younger, he wouldn't have gotten anywhere in life.

He didn't need O'Brien's permission, and his sister was old enough to make her own decisions. In fact, she presented the bigger obstacle, having told him, point-blank, they could have nothing to do with each other after the parade. Come the first of the year, she would leave for Kansas City and that was that.

He wouldn't let her get away so easily.

Above his head hung a sprig of mistletoe. The first step in his plan crystallized.

"How long before the costumes are ready?' he asked Mrs. Bowman.

"Two weeks, I'd say."

"Then we come back for a fitting?"

"That's right."

"Can you come over here a moment?" he asked the unsuspecting Miss O'Brien.

Holding his gaze warily, she approached. Over her shoulder, he saw the seamstress glance upwards, and then cover her mouth. She didn't make a sound, God bless her. Miss O'Brien hadn't noticed the mistletoe, as she had her attention trained on him.

He'd seen her watching him whenever they were together, studying him, as if trying to work out some difficult equation. He wasn't that complex but was flattered she thought so. He also took courage from her trembling response each time he touched her. It meant she was susceptible to him, and that meant he had a chance.

His heart accelerated as she drew near.

"What is it?" Her expressive eyes conveyed hesitant curiosity. He sensed she could be adventurous if he could coax her out of her disciplined shell, and get past her suspicion.

He crooked his finger, urging her closer. "After coming up with a brilliant compromise, you aren't having second thoughts are you?"

Her finely arched eyebrows drew down in a doubtful frown. "I'm still not sure why there's a need for Santa to have a wife involved. It's not part of the tradition. I've never read about a Mrs. Claus, or where she came from."

"Who's to say he didn't order her out of a newspaper?"

Miss O'Brien looked askance at what he considered a hilarious remark. The seamstress, at least, giggled.

"Thank you for agreeing to be Mrs. Claus."

"You're welcome."

God knows he owed her more than thanks. Her inspired compromise had saved his skin. Instead of donating merchandise he couldn't afford, thanks to her, all he had to do was split the cost of candy with her brother and toss in a few items for the orphans. Her project couldn't have come at a better time. However, he couldn't say that without sounding miserly, and he didn't want her to think poorly of him, or more poorly than she already did.

"You saved me a great deal of embarrassment." He could risk that much honesty.

31

Her suspicious gaze melted into sympathy. "I wouldn't have embarrassed you in front of the committee. You've been very generous."

She misunderstood because he hadn't explained, thought he meant she would've shamed him by refusing to go along as Mrs. Claus. Her concern for his feelings burrowed deep into his heart. He didn't deserve her. Then again, he hadn't deserved most of what he'd gained. The deserving rarely prospered.

"Not generous enough." He slipped his arm around her waist and bent his head. Alarm filled her eyes the instant before he covered her mouth.

She tasted of peppermint and tea, a delicious combination, somehow sweet and seductive at the same time. Holding her tight against him, he sampled the flavor on her lips, which softened and parted beneath his. He longed to linger, to feast...but not here, in front of a giggling dressmaker. He'd only intended a brief kiss, just enough to let her know what it could be like between them, as well as to make it clear to the rest of the world that he'd laid claim to her.

Regretfully, he lifted his mouth.

She blinked, dazed, and with a shocked gasp, stepped backwards, her cheeks flaming. "H-have you lost your mind?"

Perhaps. Coming to a decision as important as marriage within a few days was madly spontaneous, even for him. He hoped he wouldn't regret it, but at the moment he couldn't dredge up one ounce of caution. "Can't Santa kiss his wife under the mistletoe?"

Her horrified gaze lifted.

The seamstress gave a peculiar little snort. "He's got you there, miss. That's mistletoe. You get caught under it, and a fellow can kiss you."

The giggling recommenced.

Maggie grabbed her bag, swung her cape over her shoulders and started out the door. Before she left, she thanked Mrs. Bowman, saying she would return in two weeks to collect her costume. She would go through with this farce because she didn't back out of her commitments, but she would not spend one more minute than was necessary in Mr. Sumner's company. He'd taken advantage of her in the worst way, called her reputation into question and humiliated her after she had gone to great lengths to save him from embarrassment.

Instead of taking the sidewalk, she veered off across the park on a shortcut. Despite the cold air, her face burned. Her boots sank in the soft snow, slowing her down. She picked up her skirts and plowed a path up an incline. She'd reached the top when he caught up.

"Miss O'Brien... Margaret, wait..." He snagged her arm.

She spun around, lost her footing in the slippery snow.

With the quick instincts of a cat, he caught hold of her, halting her fall by hauling her up against his chest. However, instead of releasing her right away, as proper, he wrapped his arms around her. Out in the middle of the park, with people wandering around, watching. He would ruin her before he was through.

Panic flooded her mind, drowning out rational thought. Flailing him with her fists, she yelled, "Let go! Stop tormenting me!"

"No, wait, I'm not... Don't push me, we're on a—"

Her shove sent him backwards.

His arms circled in a windmill, as he attempted to

right himself, but then he lost his footing when he stepped back on the incline. When she reached out to save him, she ended up on top of him, and the force sent him sliding upside down to the bottom of the rise.

Somehow, he kept her from falling off. As they coasted to a stop, he began to laugh.

Maggie lifted up on trembling arms, still sprawled atop him, surprised, but not hurt. She wasn't even cold, although he must be freezing, with snow piled up around his head and shoulders. His blue eyes seemed brighter, clearer, enhanced by the heightened color in his cheeks. "Are...are you all right?" she asked breathlessly.

Still chuckling, he laid his hands on her shoulders. "I've never been a sled before. Would you like another ride?"

Saints above. Did he ever think before he spoke?

"Of all the..." She tried to get up, but got tangled in her cloak so she could only manage to roll off, and toppled onto her back. Thankfully, her hood remained up so she didn't get snow beneath her collar.

Really, it wasn't his fault she'd ended up on top of him. He had used his body as a cushion to keep her from injuring herself. Her brother had done that once, many years ago, in much difference circumstances, and with a far less amusing outcome.

Still flat on her back, she gazed into the sky, surprisingly clear and the same color blue as his eyes. How irritating that she should notice. "Mr. Sumner, you are more annoying than the worst-behaved boy in my classroom."

"No more sledding, then?" He reached for her hand and laced his gloved fingers through hers. "We could make angels in the snow if you'd prefer."

The last of her anger and frustration came out in a breathless laugh. "You must've struck your head."

"What makes you think that?"

"Because something knocked you silly."

He squeezed her hand. "Do you like me when I'm silly?"

"No."

"Do you like me when I'm serious?"

A laugh escaped in spite of her determination not to laugh, which only encouraged him. Whether she liked him or not was beyond the point. He was off limits.

Maggie untangled their fingers; holding hands with him kept her breathless. She lifted her cloaked arms to form the shape of angel wings. The childish game worked as a temporary distraction to prevent her from thinking about her attraction to the aggravating man.

He moved his arms and legs. "I haven't done this in years."

"Me neither. My students love it. I thought joining them would be beneath my dignity."

"Your secret is safe with me." He sat up, brushing the snow off the sleeves of his overcoat. With an easy hop, he got his legs under him, stood and held out his hand. "I won't tell a soul you turned me into a sled and forced me to make snow angels with you."

She tried to fight the smile, a useless effort. Sitting up, she put out her hand and let him haul her to her feet. "This isn't funny."

"Why are you laughing?" He brushed snow off her cloak. Took every opportunity to put his hands on her; and fool that she was, she actually enjoyed it, longed for him to kiss her again. This couldn't go on, something had to be done before her reputation was compromised beyond repair.

Gordon Sumner behaved outrageously, but his flirty teasing could be a cover, a defense mechanism he used to hide deep loneliness. Her peculiar sensitivity to his feelings might be because she shared them and understood how difficult it was to find the right person. In fact, she did better at matching others than she did at making her own match.

Two years ago, she'd helped her brother find Victoria. Granted, her approach had been unconventional and rather deceitful, which was something she wouldn't do again. But she'd had great success pairing him with the perfect wife. There was no reason she couldn't help Mr. Sumner, too, and in doing so, it would free her from this unwanted attraction.

She brushed loose strands of hair away from her face. By now her hair must look hopeless. "Are you in the market for a wife?"

He stared at her as if she'd suddenly blurted something in a foreign tongue.

"I've rendered you speechless. That has to be a first."

"You're not joking?"

"No at all. I'm in earnest. If you want a wife, I believe I could help you."

Beneath the snow-dampened mustache, his lips twisted in a wry smile.

"You'd better not laugh at me."

"I wouldn't dream of laughing at you." Gathering her hands, he gazed down at her with amusement and heart-rending tenderness. "Do you have someone in mind, Margaret?"

She winced at his use of her formal name. "I dislike Margaret. It sounds old."

"All right, then…Maggie." The way he said her name, low and edged with sensual promises, sent shivers racing across her skin. He'd misunderstood her intentions. He thought…

"Mr. Sumner, that's not what I—"

"Sum. It's what my friends call me."

"But we aren't friends."

He tightened his hold on her hands, reproaching her

with a look. "Of course we are. We're going to be very good friends."

Whether he'd meant to or not, he had just provided the escape she needed without getting into a discussion that would be humiliating for both of them.

"All right then, we will be friends. *Only* friends. Nothing more."

Disappointment, she'd swear it, flashed across his face before he was back to smiling. "Friends? I thought you were proposing to me. Or are we still talking pretend?"

A hot blush seared her face. "Heavens no, I'm not proposing. I meant only that I could help you search out someone who suits you. I helped my brother find Victoria." She didn't add that she'd been the one who posted the personal advertisement, wrote to the Boston miss and actually proposed, pretending to be her brother. That's not at all how she would do it again, even if everything had worked out wonderfully.

Sum gave her a puzzled, if affable, smile. "How will you help me find a wife?"

"I'll assist you with writing a personal advertisement for a bride, and you can post it in the matrimonial newspapers."

The laughter that followed made it clear he didn't take her proposition seriously.

"You want me to advertise for a bride?"

"Why do you find this so astonishing?" She folded her arms across her chest. "Hundreds of men do it, and with great success."

"You've taken a poll, then?"

"No, but I know several men who've found brides this way, my brother being one of them."

For a moment he just stood there, smiling. When she didn't respond to his amusement, his smile diminished. "You are serious."

"Very."

He didn't come back with a tart response. He might not want her help, or...

The possibility that he might actually care for her shouldn't thrill her. There could be nothing between them, not so long as he remained her brother's competitor, and he wouldn't give up his store, nor would she ask him to do so. She would find him a more appropriate wife, even if the thought made her heart ache.

Maggie drew her cape closer and shivered. The damp cold had seeped through her clothes. "If you wish to discuss it further, m-maybe we can talk about it over a cup of tea?"

He wrapped his arm around her shoulders. "I'll make a pot. Sounds like we'll need one if we're going to convince some lovely young miss that I'm the man of her dreams."

Chapter Five

Sum tried to hold on, but Maggie shied away from his arm.

"On second thought, I really should get back to help Victoria with the children. You could come over for tea later, after the store closes, and we can discuss your advertisement then."

"Very well." Growing frustrated, but not wishing to show it, he brushed the snow off his coat and walked over to pick up his hat from where it had landed after it rolled away.

He'd been having a fine time up until the point when she'd offered to find him another wife.

Being coy didn't seem to be her nature, so it would appear she couldn't wait to be rid of him. Or perhaps desperation had driven her to make the offer because she was beginning to like him. Being an optimistic fellow, he chose to believe the latter.

This diversion of hers would make courting more difficult, but he could adjust. He'd use the opportunity as an excuse to see her, and by the time they finished the ad, she would come to her senses and realize there was only one bride who met his requirements.

At five minutes past five in the evening, he crossed over to his competitor's store. The bell jangled as he entered.

O'Brien appeared to be waiting for him. He turned the sign around to *Closed* and locked the door as soon as Sum got inside. "You can use the stairs in the back. Maggie will let you in."

Sum hid his irritation behind a smile. Granted, he'd made no effort to befriend the man, and truth be told, he'd rather have a tooth pulled than spend time in O'Brien's company. For Maggie's sake, he'd attempt to make amends. He held out his hand. "Tis' the season."

The Irishman's handshake turned out to be surprisingly firm, almost painful. Maybe his annoyance stemmed from more than having to host his competitor for tea. Doubtless, Maggie had reported the outcome of their meeting with the committee, and her brother might resent being committed to spending money.

Sum flexed his hand as he withdrew it. "Thank you for pitching in on the candy for the parade. This means a great deal to Maggie."

If possible, O'Brien's expression grew darker. "You don't have to tell me what it means, and I know Maggie better than you do. Practically raised her." He turned and walked to the rear of the store with that curious gait, as if one leg might be a hair shorter than the other, hung his apron on a peg and rolled down the sleeves of his white shirt.

Sum removed his hat. The host hadn't offered to take it or his overcoat and made it clear there would be no polite conversation. Just as well. It wasn't O'Brien he'd come to see, and he wouldn't waste energy on feeling guilty about how things had worked out.

He followed the storeowner through a rear door. The storeroom looked as large as the one in the building he rented and was filled with boxes and crates, some stamped with the names of well-known manufacturers. O'Brien looked to be planning a big Christmas sale. Sum suppressed a groan. That meant another price war he couldn't afford.

"Right up there," O'Brien gestured to a stairway leading to living quarters on the second floor.

"You aren't joining us?" Sum inquired to be polite.

"Too much work to do."

Sum didn't lie and say he was disappointed. "I'll leave you to it, then."

He grasped the rail and started up the stairway. The place felt chilly. Should've left on his coat. O'Brien disappeared into a small office tucked beneath the stairs. Sum shuddered at the thought of being closeted in a windowless rat hole. Thankfully, he had plenty of room upstairs for an office. O'Brien needed the extra space for his growing family.

Sum slowed as he reached the landing. When he and Maggie married and had children, they would need more living space. That would be a while, enough time to resolve debts and start saving so he could expand, or better yet, purchase a proper house. With more than one to provide for, he'd have to be more frugal. That didn't mean he had to scrimp on coal to heat the place.

Facing the door, Sum smoothed down his hair, checked the bow tie and then switched his overcoat and hat to his left hand and knocked with his right.

After a moment, the door opened and a young girl gazed up at him. She could've been an eight-year-old version of Maggie. He'd seen the child around, but he'd never been struck by the thought that he might enjoy having a daughter with luminous dark eyes and sable braids.

His breathing became constricted. He cleared his

41

throat and made a bow. "Good evening, Miss Fannie. I'm Mr. Sumner."

"Aunt Maggie told me you'd be here. She's in the kitchen with Mama. She said to let you in and tell you to sit down and wait."

"Were those her precise words?"

Fannie's raven brows gathered in thought. "She might've said something else, but I forget."

Fighting laughter, Sum followed the girl inside. The apartment setup appeared similar to his, with a large parlor flanked by bedrooms in the back and a kitchen and dining area in the front.

He smelled something sweet baking, mingled with a woodsy scent. *Pine.* Coming from a Christmas tree tucked into a corner. On its dark green boughs hung a hodgepodge of decorations, a combination of store-bought ornaments and handmade treasures. The cozy family room, with its worn upholstery and intriguing scents, had an inviting atmosphere that his well-appointed rooms lacked. Must be the Christmas tree. That was another thing he'd need to add to the list after Maggie moved in.

"You've put up a tree," he noted to his short hostess. "That reminds me, I'll need to get busy and put mine up, too."

Fannie crossed to a stuffed chair pushed aside to make room for the tree and picked up a doll, which looked to be a miniature of a child her age, only blond and blue-eyed. She flounced onto the chair and swung her feet. Her shoes had gone missing and her woolen stockings, visible by several inches beneath her plaid frock, sagged around her ankles.

"Alice helped me make the angels," she explained in a mature tone. "Patrick tried, but he kept eating the crepe paper and Mama had to put him to bed."

Sum smoothed his mustache to hide his amusement.

Fannie wasn't trying to be funny. "After eating crepe paper, I should think I would want to crawl into bed, too."

"Is Fannie keeping you entertained?" Maggie entered the parlor, carrying a tray with a tea set and two cups. She'd changed into a crisp striped shirtwaist and dark wool skirt. Her pretty velvet suit must've gotten damp from rolling around in the snow. Maybe she'd mentioned something about their mishap to her brother and that's why he was so out of sorts.

"Miss Fannie is an excellent hostess," Sum assured Maggie.

"That's good to hear. We'll have warm sugar cookies out in just a minute."

Catching Fannie's eye, he put his hand to his middle and smacked his lips. "My stomach's growling already."

"Mine, too!" Fannie hopped down with the doll hugged to her chest. "Alice wants a cookie, so I'll have to get two," she informed her aunt.

Maggie nodded agreeably. "Of course. We wouldn't want to deprive Alice."

Fannie skipped off to the kitchen, he assumed to make sure she and Alice received their due.

Maggie set the tray on a table in front of the sofa, which appeared to have been shortened to make it suitable for serving coffee or tea to guests. Most of the furniture in the room reflected a popular mid-century style, overly fussy in his opinion. It might not be Maggie's choice, being her brother's home. Her clothing reflected simpler tastes, less flamboyant. Sum hoped she liked Eastlake's designs. Redecorating wasn't in his budget.

She took his coat and hat, hanging both on the hall tree, and after pouring tea, fled to a wing-backed chair closest to the sofa. This would be so much easier if she would cooperate.

"You might sit over here…" He put his hand on the sofa cushion as he sat down. "Easier to compare notes on the advertisement."

Maggie placed her cup and saucer on the marble tabletop next to her chair. "I can discuss it from here. Once I know what you're looking for, I'll put something on paper and you can come back tomorrow to take a look."

Little minx thought to avoid being alone with him.

"Not during the day, too busy. After the stores close, you can stop by and we'll have time to work on it together." Sum picked up the teacup, having to pinch the delicate little handle to hold it. Rather than risk dumping hot tea in his lap, he cradled the china base.

She peered suspiciously over the rim of her cup as she took a sip. "You could come over here."

And face her glowering Irish guardian again? *No, thank you.*

He shook his head. "It's bad enough we're disturbing your family tonight. You don't wish to do that every night. The parade is only two weeks away. We need time to discuss revisions to the parade posters, and a newspaper article, maybe a column from Mrs. Claus about the orphans and what they need. We can work on my personal advertisement in between."

Maggie sat straight in the chair with her best schoolmarm expression. "David and Victoria don't mind. If it bothers you to meet here, we'll use the store. There's a counter down there where we can spread out."

"My store has a larger counter, and less noise." He glanced meaningfully in the direction of the laughter coming from the kitchen. "That's only from one, the louder one hasn't roused from his nap yet."

She didn't have an immediate comeback.

Sum restrained the urge to throw his hands up in the air, declaring the winner. Round one had gone to him.

He'd win the next round, too. Not on brute strength—he'd learned quickly in a short-lived stint in the ring that he wouldn't get far with his fists. He won more often by using his wits, and when it came to Maggie, he'd need to exercise a fair amount of self-control. At least, as long as he could hold out until he got the chance to kiss her again.

Maggie tensed, facing off with Sum. Noise aside, his point about bothering her brother and sister-in-law had merit. Sometimes she felt like an interloper. David had his own family and didn't really need her anymore. Before remarrying, her brother had depended on her to help him with Fannie, and she had put aside a teaching career for two years to assist him. He'd done so much for her, she wanted to do what she could for him, which was why she'd sent off for a mail-order bride on his behalf.

Sum didn't need to order a bride if he could find one locally. She might be able to come up with a suggestion, once she knew what he considered suitable. Either way, she wasn't letting the sly fox coerce her into being alone with him again.

"Cookies anyone?" Victoria announced, entering the room with a platter of warm treats in the shape of Santa Claus. They'd used one of the new cookie-cutters David had ordered and then sold out of within a fortnight.

Maggie set her cup aside. "Umm, they smell delicious."

"Of course they do. You made them." Victoria set the platter on the table in front of Sum. "Maggie would never brag, but she's the one who taught me how to cook. My cookies aren't nearly as good as hers. She's also a master at pies and cakes...and biscuits." Victoria tossed an amused glance over her shoulder. "Isn't that right?"

Maggie loved how her sister-in-law could laugh at herself. "Your biscuits have gotten much better since that first time."

"I should hope so." Victoria handed a cookie on a napkin to their guest. "My first attempt at cooking biscuits resulted in nearly burning the building down."

"Oh, now that's not so." Maggie found the memory of the incident amusing, though at the time it had been anything but. "You didn't come close to burning anything down. It was just smoky."

"Coal chips," Victoria declared. "That's what my first biscuits looked like."

"How did they taste?" Sum's polite inquiry elicited laughter.

"They were *awful*." Fannie sidled up to Victoria, who wrapped an arm around her and gave her a hug. The sweet affection between the two, forged through Victoria's patience and persistence, put a lump in Maggie's throat. She missed her niece something fierce but was glad Victoria had become Fannie's mother and given David another child. Maggie wasn't sure what Sum would be looking for, but this, this kind of love, that's what she wanted.

His questioning gaze met hers, like he'd picked up on her thoughts, but then he returned his attention to Fannie, scrunching his nose in an exaggerated expression of distaste. "You ate the coal chips?"

Fannie went into a fit of giggles. "They were biscuits...and no, we didn't *eat* them...not even Alice would eat them."

Sum leaned forward, as if intrigued. "What does Alice like to eat?"

Fannie eyed the platter longingly. "Oh, she loves Christmas cookies."

"If it's permissible, she may have half of mine." Sum broke the cookie in two and held it out. The charmer. He would win Fannie's heart, as well.

Victoria nodded her approval. "Put it in the kitchen, then, to save for after dinner."

She brushed her hands off on her apron. Her hips were slender, even augmented with a bustle. Still, she had an enviable figure. Did Sum prefer willowy women or full-figured ones?

Maggie glanced down at her oh-so-average form. Looking up, she met his gaze, and blushed. Saints above, had he seen her examining her bosom?

Fannie inched toward Sum to retrieve her prize. For some reason, she appeared reticent to approach him, even though she'd had her eyes on him the entire time. She might think it strange that a man had come by to see her Aunt Maggie.

Heaven knows her callers had been few and far between. Then again, she hadn't found a man she wanted to encourage, not until she'd met the one man she shouldn't encourage.

Her niece took half the cookie out of Sum's hand. "My Da says you aren't nice—"

"Fannie!" Victoria called sharply, at the same time Maggie sucked in a sharp breath. Maybe the child didn't realize she'd offended Sum because David had made disparaging remarks in her presence. It was time to put an end to that.

Sum didn't react like a man who'd been insulted. In fact, he smiled kindly at Fannie. "Your father must've read the naughty list and seen a name that looked like mine."

Maggie breathed easier.

Victoria managed to hide her displeasure behind a cool façade. "Fannie, please take the cookie into the kitchen, and then I'd like for you to meet me in your room."

Fannie's eyes grew wide and bright with tears. "I didn't mean to do anything wrong."

"Don't fear, your name isn't on a naughty list," Sum assured her. "Old St. Nick allowed me to help out this year for the parade, and I've checked. You're definitely not on that list with the other naughty children, and neither is Alice."

Faith, what a sweet man... Maggie withheld her applause. Had she been sitting next to him, she might've given him a hug.

Fannie offered him a tremulous smile before obediently heading into the kitchen.

Victoria waited until Fannie had completed her task and disappeared down the hallway and they heard the sound of her door closing. "Thank you, Mr. Sumner, for your kindness. I hope you'll accept my apology on behalf of my daughter...and my husband."

"No need to apologize," Sum replied in his usual friendly tone.

Victoria excused herself and went after Fannie. As soon as she left the room, he stood.

"Probably best if I leave," he said.

So he had been offended but was too much of a gentleman to admit it.

Maggie came to her feet. "I'm so sorry." She followed him to the door, retrieving his coat and hat. What a fiasco. She should never have invited him to her brother's home, not with the high probability of conflict. "Please forgive me for bringing you here, and causing you embarrassment."

Sum's smile turned rueful. "If I'm suffering from embarrassment, I have no one to blame but myself. Fannie's right. I haven't been nice to your brother. That's something I intend to correct—within the bounds of friendly competition."

Maggie's eyes stung at a sudden welling of gratitude.

There had been a time when she'd viewed him as poorly as David did. Sum had proved them wrong. Today, he'd handled an uncomfortable situation with humor and understanding, and put Fannie at ease. He would make a good Santa, being easy to approach and good with children. He didn't have any, as far as she knew, but then again, she knew very little about him. She must get to know him better, in order to write his advertisement, of course. That meant she would need to go to him.

"I'll be over tomorrow to discuss the article for the parade." She handed him his coat.

"And you promised to help me with a personal advertisement, don't forget that." He maintained a straight face, so she couldn't tell if he intended the remark as a joke, or simply as a reminder. Either way, she didn't back out on commitments, and she was determined to find this remarkable man a very good match.

"I haven't forgotten. I'll write something up, and you can take a look at it. We want it to be perfect."

"If you're writing it, I'm sure it will be." He replaced his hat, tugging the brim in a brief farewell. He didn't kiss her.

She shouldn't have been surprised...or disappointed.

Chapter Six

The week before Christmas couldn't have started out more perfectly, in Sum's opinion. Shoppers turned out in hoards and sales were better than ever. The parade costumes had been finished on time. Best of all, Maggie would arrive at any moment.

Sum checked the pot of tea on the stove. His personal preference was coffee, but he'd take up tea if it meant he could drink it with Maggie.

He'd spent a blissful two weeks in her company. Each evening after the stores closed, she would come over to work on parade posters and nitpick his article about the fundraising drive. Each time she brought up the personal advertisement, he put off discussing it. If things progressed as he hoped, he wouldn't need it.

One night, Victoria O'Brien had invited him to dinner. Her husband remained polite, if not talkative, perhaps deciding he shouldn't say anything if he couldn't say something nice. Maggie acted nervous. To relieve her tension, Sum spun tales about Santa Claus and his wife and the reindeer and everything else he could recall reading about the *jolly old elf*. He succeeded in making Maggie and Victoria laugh, and even David O'Brien started to smile.

The fact that he'd be concerned about gaining the good opinion of his competitor confirmed his pathetic condition. The worst part, he didn't mind taking the head-over-heels tumble and had no interest in getting over it. He hadn't planned on this, wouldn't have gone out looking to catch it, but ever since Maggie had come into his life, he couldn't imagine going on without her.

A knock sounded. She was never late. That was a good sign. Try as she might to hide it, he could tell she was as eager to be with him as he was to be with her. This nonsense about finding him a bride was just her quirky way of resisting the inevitable. He adored her quirks.

He opened the door, and a swirl of cold air followed her inside. "Come in and get warm."

She drew back her hood. "It is warm in here. You must use more fuel than David does."

Sum frowned, not liking the image of her shivering in the cold. "He allows you to freeze?"

"Of course not. He's just frugal. I can always put on a coat."

Maggie turned to allow him to take her heavy cloak. She'd pulled her thick hair up with combs, leaving a few silky curls to escape down the back of her neck. He couldn't resist a quick kiss just below her hairline.

She whirled around, startled. "No kisses, we agreed."

"Did we? I don't recall." He wasn't promising any such thing.

Her fingers moved up the tiny jet buttons on a fitted jacket, as if she were checking to make sure each one remained fastened. He imagined undoing them and following the trail with his lips.

God, he burned for her, and she wanted him as well. All signs pointed to it: her eagerness to be with him, her secret smiles and adorable blushes, the way she watched from beneath her lashes when she thought he wasn't looking.

"No more kisses," she said sternly. "I have my reputation to protect, and you'll soon be marrying someone else."

Her remark didn't fool him. It did, however, irritate him. She kept insisting they were just friends, reminding him that after the first of the year she would go back to her teaching job in Kansas City and he would send off for his bride.

The only bride he wanted was Maggie. Whatever the obstacle—be it her brother, her job, or her own uncertainty—he would overcome it. Nothing would stand in the way of getting what he wanted, not even Maggie.

"Come sit down. I'll pour you a cup of tea." He ushered her to the rear of the store where he'd set cups out on the counter. She refused to go upstairs to his office or apartment, for propriety's sake. Fine, he'd wait until they were married to bed her.

"Are you hungry?"

She settled onto a stool and adjusted her skirts. "I had dinner before I came over. No need for you to feed me."

Why not? It was an excellent idea, slipping her morsels in between kisses...something to look forward to.

She fished out a folded sheet of paper and a pencil from a serviceable leather bag she'd placed on the counter. "I took the liberty of working on the advertisement..."

Sum poured tea into two cups. He unbuttoned the front of his tweed coat and took the neighboring stool. Seeing as she wouldn't be dissuaded, he would play along. "Can't wait to hear what you've come up with."

Maggie's attention remained on the paper. She

smoothed it out on the counter and studied it, almost too intently. Annoying, how she refused to look at him. He could make her notice.

With his forefinger, he smoothed a silken strand away from her face. The touch drew a reprimanding look, which softened at his smile.

"You take too many liberties." She scolded in a voice too soft for her to be put out.

"Do I?" He considered taking more, such as drawing her to him and kissing her thoroughly. But then she would accuse him of violating his promise and that would give her a convenient way out. No, he had to remain patient. Seduce her by inches, not yards.

Without apology, he picked up his cup and took a drink. He'd work with her on this silly advertisement and in the process make her admit she was his perfect match. At least, that was the plan. His biggest worry—his plans, like his father's, had a way of going awry. He wouldn't allow that to happen this time. "Read what you've written so far."

"Successful merchant in fast-growing Western community seeks educated young woman with exemplary reputation for purposes of marriage. Applicant must be willing to work long days and will need patience—"

He laughed, nearly spitting his tea, and set down the cup. "Patience? Am I that trying?

"You didn't let me finish. *Will need patience with children.*" She glanced at him with a wry smile. "I assume you'll want children, and your wife will need patience if you expect her to work in a store and look after them."

Her assumption would've been wrong a mere few weeks ago. "Children? When did I start wanting those?"

"I don't know." Maggie searched his eyes, as if she'd find an answer there. She would if she looked very hard. "Have you been married before? Did you have other children?"

"Never married. No children." None that he knew of, and he'd been careful.

"Was it after you agreed to play Santa?"

"That decision had nothing to do with children, entirely selfish; I wanted to wear the green robe." He loved the little flutter and eye roll she did when he made a joke.

"Maybe it was after you met Fannie?"

"Your niece's bluntness endeared her to me, but no, it had to be after I met you."

"Ah, because I'm a schoolteacher." Maggie sidestepped his blatant admission with admirable dexterity. She must be practicing at home.

Undaunted, Sum gazed into her eyes. This close, he could see they weren't black, but a deep, rich brown, the way he liked his coffee. "What about how she looks?"

Maggie's lips parted like she might say something, but forgot what it was. She jerked her attention to the sheet of paper on the counter. "You mean to say, you want an *attractive* bride. We can add that. Remember, the personal advertisements run forty words. It'll cost you extra for every word thereafter."

"We're not to forty words yet." Didn't matter, at any rate. By the time he finished listing his requirements, there would be no question in her mind as to which bride he wanted.

She sighed, and picked up the pencil. "I haven't even gotten to the part about you."

"I like what you wrote about me being a successful merchant." That's what he wanted her to believe, and it would be so, once he'd cleared his debts. He saw no reason to enlighten her as to his current financial instability. She might let something slip. Not to hurt him, but because she seemed to think her brother would qualify as a saint.

She bent over the paper and scribbled something. "The difficulty in writing a personal advertisement is effectively selling yourself while remaining completely honest."

Sum leaned in and inhaled her scent. "Honest, yes... You smell of peppermint."

Maggie glanced at him with alarm and slanted away. She reached into a pocket on her jacket. "I forgot I had these in here. Would you like one?"

He plucked a red and white candy out of her palm. "Thank you. I love peppermints."

"You do? They're my favorite."

"Mine, too." They'd become his favorite ever since he'd started associating the smell with Maggie. Who knew candy could be so provocative? He would keep a jar in their bedroom. "Include that in the advertisement. Favorite candy must be peppermint."

She laughed, revealing white teeth that were, for the most part, even. One tooth near the front slightly overlapped another. The imperfection endeared her to him even more. He couldn't meet the standards of a perfect woman. "Sum, be serious. Only include what's most important."

He rolled the sweet minty candy around in his mouth, remembering the taste on her lips. "That's pretty important, don't you think?"

"I can think of other things more important."

"Such as?"

Maggie lifted her cup and blew across the tea, sending ripples over the dark surface, before taking a careful sip. That he found everything she did fascinating concerned him because she didn't appear to suffer from the same condition. He could tell she liked him and even desired him, but as for being smitten... Well, if she'd fallen, she did a good job hiding it.

She set her cup down and picked up the pencil. "We

need to list your good traits so your bride knows what she's getting."

That would be a short list. "You said I was successful."

"That's not a trait."

He ventured out on a limb. "What, in your opinion, are my good traits?"

She tapped the pencil on her pursed lips. Perhaps that helped her think. He hoped she didn't have to think too hard to come up with something.

"Your sense of humor," she said at last. "It's not always proper, but you can make me laugh, even when I'm vexed with you."

"That's self-preservation."

She smiled, and wrote *witty* on the paper. More words followed: *engaging, affectionate, generous…*

He felt each stroke of the pen across his heart. "Are those traits appealing enough?"

"I would think so, but I'm not the one you need to convince."

"Your opinion matters." In fact, her opinion was the only one that mattered.

She ignored another clear hint and went on. "We need to describe you. You'll send a photograph, but that doesn't tell her the color of your hair or eyes."

He made a face. "I thought you said this list needed to impress her."

"You know you have impressive looks, don't act so humble."

His lips tugged into a foolish smile at her praise. He did try to make the best of what God had given him, but he had never considered his looks *impressive*. "Some women don't appreciate red hair."

"Your hair isn't red. It's…" She eyed the top of his head. "It's more the color of sassafras leaves in the fall. Only deeper, richer."

He passed his hand over his hair. Up until this moment, he'd despised the color. "I've never heard my red hair described quite that way.

Maggie shook her head at him. "I told you, it's not red. More of a deep orange with rich umber tones, auburn perhaps, though I don't think that word does it justice. And your eyes aren't just blue. They're the color of a winter sky after the clouds have cleared and the sun comes out."

His heart lodged in his throat. She couldn't describe him in those soaring terms and not want him. "What about her traits?"

"We listed those. Educated, hard-working, patient, attractive…"

"That's not specific enough."

"All right, then. What specifically do you want?"

Now, he would make his requirements crystal clear, and they could stop this nonsense about mail-order brides. Although if she wanted to wax poetic about his looks, he'd encourage her, preferably while they lay in bed together.

Holding her gaze, he reached out and captured a curl dangling near her ear. "She has to have black hair that glistens and feels like silk, and gypsy eyes, dark as coffee."

Maggie's gaze widened. Her delicate nostrils flared, and her tongue slipped out to moisten her lips, all signs of sensual awareness and mutual desire. Her reaction made his body tense and his heart pound harder.

She shook herself and batted his hand away. "Stop this." Her expression shifted from angry to anxious to regretful. "You aren't making it any easier by teasing me."

Sum's smile fell away. To hell with these games. He grasped her arms and drew her to him. "Who's teasing? You asked for my requirements."

Before he could kiss her, Maggie turned her face. His lips landed on her cheek. Without missing a beat, he blazed a trail to her ear. "Write it down," he whispered. "Then add that I want her to smell like peppermint, and to roll her eyes at my jokes, and go along with my crazy scheme to put Mrs. Claus in the parade—"

She slammed her eyes shut, but that didn't block out his words, or keep her skin from shivering as his breath gusted in the shell of her ear. He delicately traced the edge with the tip of his tongue, sending another spasm of quivers rippling through her.

"Please, Sum...stop...I don't want this..." Liar. She wanted him more than she'd wanted anyone or anything.

"You do want this, so do I." His mouth moved to her neck and he grazed his teeth against her sensitized flesh.

Her shivers became trembles, and an urgent ache started somewhere deep in her core. She couldn't break free of his tight grip on her arms without dragging them both off the stools, and the possibility of ending up on the floor on her back put the fear of God into her. Desperate, she braced her hands on his heaving chest, trying to push him away so he'd stop tormenting her.

"For the love of St. Michael," she whispered.

"Gordon," he murmured, "and I'm not a saint."

Blasphemous sinner. She should've heeded the signs, ever since he'd kissed her under the mistletoe. However, this wasn't flirting or teasing, he was doing his level best to seduce her. She stammered, trying to remind him, to remind herself, they had agreed to be only friends. "You...we...we can't be..."

When his hands moved upward and into her hair, she

somehow found the strength to leap off the stool. She backed away, reaching up with shaking hands to keep her hair from falling. The devil had taken her combs.

He dropped the heavy tortoise shell combs on the counter and advanced toward her, looking every inch the predator she'd once imagined him to be. Beyond the sensual heat in his eyes gleamed another emotion, one that looked like desperation. He held out his arms. "Maggie, why are you resisting what's between us? I know you feel it. I feel it, too."

She shook her head. "No, I can't become your...your concubine, and face myself in the mirror."

"Concubine? Where do you find these words?" He huffed a soft laugh, sounding incredulous. "You think I'm asking you to be my mistress? I wouldn't dishonor you, Maggie. Good God, woman, I all but dictated your measurements for that bride advertisement."

Her resistance wavered.

Sum had her in his arms before she could blink. He must've sensed her weakness, and pounced. His mouth silenced her protest.

The moment his lips touched hers, the fire inside reignited. Ablaze, she wound her arms around his neck and she kissed him with all the pent-up longing in her heart. He wanted her, she wanted him, and in this moment, nothing else mattered.

She didn't fight when he dug his fingers into her hair, pulling her head back so he could trail hot kisses down her neck. He murmured love words mixed with obscene suggestions, but the way he said them didn't sound repulsive.

He returned to worship her mouth while at the same time moving his hands over her, stroking her back, following the swell of her hips, his every touch taking her to greater heights. "You know we're meant to be together," he murmured against her lips.

Yes, she knew they'd fit like puzzle pieces, their bodies and their hearts. That thought triggered an abrupt return to reality. If she gave Sum her heart, it would be the ultimate betrayal of her brother. Torn loyalties would tear her apart.

Squelching her selfishness, she pulled away, and before Sum could stop her, rushed to the counter, scooping her combs into her bag. Springing away from him, she grabbed her cloak. "I have to leave."

"The hell you will." Glowing with frustration, he stopped her at the door, dropped to one knee and grasped her free hand. "Marry me." He didn't ask. He demanded.

Her head grew light, and she feared she might swoon—for the first time in her life. "Sum, I...I..."

He gazed up with an intensity she'd never seen before. "We get along famously, and I know I could make you happy...if you'd let me."

His plea tightened a vise around her heart. She tried to find her voice so she could plead with him not to beg for her hand, tell him she wasn't worth crushing his pride. Her vision blurred as tears gathered along her lower lids. "I'm honored, so very honored, I can't express how much it means to me. But, I can't accept."

His face grew stiff. "Yes, you *can*. Don't let anything stand in the way of what you want."

She couldn't act that way, and if he could, then maybe they didn't belong together. The painful realization sent streams coursing down her cheeks. "I could never betray my brother by marrying a man who could put him out of business."

Sum stood, looming over her. "This isn't about your brother. Whether or not his business survives isn't up to you."

"I'm not talking about his business." Her voice cracked with emotion. She tried to stop crying, but it was no use, her heart was breaking. "This is about love, loyalty, being part of a family."

The fierceness in Sum's expression softened. He cupped her face, wiping the tears away with his thumbs. "That's what I'm offering you, a family. You said you were orphaned."

She clasped his wrists, meaning to pull his hands away, but instead she clung to him. "Orphaned, yes, but I wasn't alone. My brother took care of me. Didn't someone take care of you?"

His gaze turned glacial. "No, I took care of myself. My father was too busy chasing his wild ideas. My mother never came out of her self-pity long enough to notice I was around. My brothers died when I was four."

Every word fell like a hammer blow to her heart. "I didn't know. I'm sorry."

"Don't be sorry. It's not your fault, and I didn't tell you that to gain your pity. Not sure why I blurted it out. Maybe because you keep talking about family as if everyone has one."

She had grown up painfully aware that not one everyone had a family. Her brother had been the only family she had for years, and she didn't remember much about their lives beforehand. Except, she knew they'd been loved. Sum hadn't even had that much. No wonder he grasped at affection and held onto it so tightly. He was afraid to let go, fearful no one would be there for him. This painful letting go, it was her fault. She'd let him believe she could be his family.

"Please forgive me," she whispered.

His angry frown turned to one of unhappy confusion. His hands fell away from her face. Then he dug a handkerchief out of his vest pocket and offered it to her. "Here, I always carry a clean one in case I happen across a crying woman."

"Thank you." She dried her eyes. He'd offered her far

more than a handkerchief, but that was all she could accept. However, she owed him more than gratitude. She owed him honesty.

"I wish things could be different, with all my heart I do. But David would never do anything to hurt me, and he knows I would never betray him, and it would be a terrible betrayal if I married you. It's bad enough we've become friends."

"Our friendship is bad? So you'll end that, too?" The hurt in Sum's eyes sent pain knifing through her. Couldn't he understand she had no choice except to cut the ties?

She gathered her cloak around her, and with it her resolve. "You must see, we can't be friends anymore. Not now. We can't be anything to each other."

He opened the door, his movements jerky, and when he turned to her, his gaze had hardened. "Good night, Maggie. I'll see you the day of the parade."

Chapter Seven

Snow fell early on the day of the parade. A soft white blanket covered the streets and sidewalks and collected in canopies and on tree branches. Come noon, the festivities would commence, with or without clear skies. Life went on, regardless of storms.

Maggie stood in her brother's store next to a Christmas tree he'd put on display and stared across the street. Sum wouldn't open his store for another hour. He and David both opened at eight, and, until recently, had closed at exactly the same time. They offered many of the same goods, priced them similarly. There was no need for two stores. One would fold, eventually. Regardless of which one failed, her heart would break.

She held the handkerchief he'd given her to her face, inhaling the clean smell of soap along with a faint masculine scent. A fierce yearning wrung her heart. She'd never meant to hurt Gordon Sumner. She hadn't meant to fall in love with him, either. But she'd done both, and now she didn't know what to do. The only thing she could do was to go on as if nothing changed, even if everything had changed.

At a noise behind her, she tucked the hankie beneath the hem of her sleeve and turned.

Her niece had entered the store from the back. She held her little brother's hand, steadying the toddler as he walked. Fannie's crimson velvet dress featured a frilly apron. Patrick's outfit with its wide lace collar made him look like a miniature Little Lord Fauntleroy, the character from one of Victoria's favorite books.

Maggie put on a delighted face. She wouldn't ruin this day for the children by focusing on her misery. "Oh my, look at the two of you. You're all ready for the parade."

Patrick babbled something incomprehensible.

Fannie gaped at her. "You look just like Mrs. Claus, Aunt Maggie."

She meant the image Sum had suggested over dinner one night when he'd told the children a story about Santa and his missus. There were no pictures Maggie knew of that showed a Mrs. Claus. Sum had also dictated the dress design, which had turned out beautifully. She would thank him when she saw him later this morning. She dreaded the moment as much as she longed for it.

Maggie smiled and curtseyed, holding out a berry red skirt to reveal gold and white petticoats. The sleeves and collar were trimmed with lace, as was the bonnet. "Why, I am Mrs. Claus. Who's Aunt Maggie?"

Fannie giggled.

Patrick teetered as he struck out on his own. Maggie scooped him into her arms and gave him a kiss on his pudgy cheek. He patted her hair, and powder filled the air.

"Your hair is dusty," Fannie pointed out.

"Dusty?" Maggie captured Patrick's hand before he could ruin her coiffure. "My hair is gray, dear. I'm not a spring chicken."

"Kee," Patrick said.

"She's not a kitty, either," Fannie replied. She seemed to have a fine grasp on Patrick's unique language, even if his logic didn't make sense. "When will Santa Claus be here?"

"Not until ten," her father replied. David passed by the potbellied stove without stopping to add fuel. Sum always made sure his store remained toasty.

"Why don't you add a bit more wood?" Maggie suggested. "Make it warmer. The air is very chilly, and I'm sure the children are cold."

David returned to the stove and adjusted the dampers. "Feels the same as it always does. No one's complained." He didn't add, *except you.*

Maggie secured Patrick's little coat, battling a surprising surge of resentment with a good dose of reason. It wasn't so cold the children would get ill. David made sure of that. He was just thrifty. Sum's extravagance with fuel could be a sign that he was wasteful. Except, he hadn't wasted a single moment of time they'd been together. He'd filled every minute with wonderful memories.

She set Patrick down, not wanting the children to see her tears. "Here, Fannie. Can you take him before he pats all the powder out of my hair? It's making my eyes water."

"Yes, Aunt Maggie. I mean, Mrs. Claus."

David held out a handful of peppermint candies. "We finished putting the bags of candy together. I saved some extra peppermints for you."

"You smell of peppermint…I love peppermint."

Maggie caught a sharp breath as Sum's voice slipped into her thoughts. The tears started up again. Alarmed, she spun around and made for the front door. "No, thank you. I'd rather you save it for the children." Her voice came out wobbly, but at least she didn't break down. "I should see if Santa's sleigh has arrived yet."

Before she reached the knob, her brother's hand fell on her shoulder. "The door is still locked. It's not even eight."

She bit her lip. Shuddered. Teetered on the edge of control.

"Fannie, take Patrick with you and go find your mother." David's voice resonated in the quiet store. After a moment, he put both hands on Maggie's shoulders and gave a gentle squeeze. "The children are gone," he said softly.

She turned into his arms, fighting tears. "I'm sorry. I've been very emotional of late. I...I'm worried about collecting enough gifts for the orphans. It would be terrible if some of them were left out."

He patted her back in a big brotherly fashion. "They won't be. I spoke with the other merchants, and they've promised to cover any shortfall. You won't have to depend on Sumner. He's made promises he can't deliver on, I suspect."

She stiffened at her brother's critical tone. "Mr. Sumner will do his part, I'm sure."

"Maggie..." David spoke her name low and urgent. "Tell me what happened between you and Sumner the other night. That's what this is about, isn't it? What did he do to you?"

She drew back, under better control now, and met her brother's worried gaze. "If you must know, he proposed."

"He *what?*" David's angry reaction was to be expected.

"Don't get upset. I turned him down." Maggie swallowed the thickness in her throat. She couldn't let on that she was heartbroken, or give any sign of regretting her decision.

"Why did you turn Mr. Sumner down?" Victoria's question came from the back of the store.

David turned abruptly. "Why wouldn't she turn him down? He's an unprincipled rascal."

Sum wasn't a rascal, most of the time, and he had a deep core of honor, despite a few questionable practices, such as kissing her in public.

Before she could speak, Victoria replied. "I didn't ask your opinion of him, David. I want to hear what Maggie thinks. She's spent quite a lot of time with him lately."

"Only because he tricked her into being part of the parade," her husband shot back.

"From what I heard, she volunteered."

"Are you defending Sumner?"

Oh dear, David hadn't frowned like that at Victoria since she'd forgiven him for being a nincompoop and put him out of his misery by marrying him.

"I'm not defending anyone, except Maggie." Victoria planted her hands on her hips. She took that position when she was put out, or prepared to go to war.

Maggie groaned. Pitting her brother and sister-in-law against each other was exactly what she did *not* want to do. She stepped between them with a confession. "Yes, I have been spending time with Mr. Sumner, and we...we've become friends."

In spite of what she'd told him, she still considered him her friend. When—or if—he got around to forgiving her, he might consider her a friend as well. She hoped they could go back to being friendly acquaintances, if she could bear seeing him without bursting into tears.

"He's not a rascal, David. He's a very nice man. But, he's not the right man for me."

Her brother gave a satisfied nod. "There you go. She's told you what she thinks."

Victoria dropped her battle stance. "If you don't return Mr. Sumner's affections, then you did the right thing by ending it." She didn't sound as if she believed this to be the case.

"No, I can't return his affections..." Spinning the truth out of joint turned out to be more difficult than Maggie expected. The truth, however, was too frightening to consider. She couldn't be in love with a man she barely knew, not even if he did make her heart race.

Victoria had entered the store, trailed by the children. Fannie peered from around her back. Patrick had dropped to his knees to examine something on the floor and almost had it in his mouth when his mother scooped him up. She tugged a length of string out of his chubby fist and took him to David. "He's developed an appetite for anything that might choke him. Will you watch him while I help Maggie fix her hair?"

That was secret code for "*let's have a talk.*"

"The store opens soon. Don't be bending Maggie's ear for too long."

Apparently, David had cracked the code.

He took Patrick into his arms and ruffled his son's hair.

Maggie's breath caught at the tender gesture. She couldn't help thinking about how much she'd love to have a little boy with flaming hair and crystal blue eyes.

"Fannie?" Victoria held up the string. "The cats might enjoy this."

"I'll take it to them." Fannie wound the string around her finger and pattered back to the storeroom where the two cats prowled when they weren't curled up by the stove.

"Will you come upstairs with me for a minute?" Victoria asked. "We won't be long. Patrick messed up your hair. I'll fix it."

Maggie knew her sister-in-law was too tactful to challenge her decision or outright tell her what she should do, something her older brother considered his prerogative. Victoria expressed her concern in a less direct manner. Nevertheless, Maggie didn't want to talk about Sum.

"My hair is fine." Maggie checked the watch pinned to her bodice. "It's almost time to go."

Victoria conceded with a dignified nod. "Are you ready, then?"

No, she wasn't ready to face Sum. Her heart was too raw, her emotions too close to the surface. She felt like a snowflake in a blizzard. It terrified her to think she couldn't stop what had been put into motion when she'd walked into Sumner's store to ask for his assistance.

David carried his son to the front door and unlocked it. "Let's take a peek outside and see if we spy any reindeer."

Patrick squirmed to the get down. His eyes were on the shiny ornaments that dangled from a Christmas tree forming the centerpiece of a window display. Rather than risk disaster, David lifted the child to his shoulders. Patrick grabbed his father's hair and rocked excitedly on his favorite perch. He yanked so hard that David took told of his hands.

"You're his favorite horse," Maggie quipped.

David bounced, giving his son a gleeful ride, although he wasn't smiling. "You're wise to stay away from Sumner. He's vain and self-centered. Not a man you can depend on."

Maggie's temper flared into a full-fledged blaze. She faced her brother with her hands on her hips, in battle position. "Why do you feel the need to criticize him? He's done nothing worse than move in across the street and open a shop. There's no law that says he can't do that."

Her brother gaped at her as if a holly bush had suddenly sprouted from her head.

She was just getting started. She'd not allow David to make Sum out to be a scoundrel because he wasn't a scoundrel.

"He runs a successful business. Even you have learned from watching him." She raised her hands to gesture to the interior of the store, which had over the past two years been expanded and improved with new lighting, wider aisles and prices clearly marked on merchandise. "One could say you took his best ideas, benefited from his knowledge."

"David didn't take anything." Victoria came to her husband's defense and to his side. Her expression remained polite, but her tone had a sharp edge. "Mr. Sumner doesn't own those concepts. He's doing what stores in the east have been doing for several years, which I suggested David might try."

Maggie wasn't surprised or offended by her sister-in-law's protective streak, which extended to her as well. David didn't really need protecting, with the exception of his hair.

Victoria retrieved Patrick before the toddler snatched his father bald-headed. She lovingly combed her fingers through her husband's mussed hair. "Maggie, you know your brother wouldn't steal from anyone."

David grasped Victoria's wrist, pulled her closer and pressed a quick kiss on her lips, making her blush. "Except for kisses. I steal those all the time."

Their easy affection usually made Maggie happy, but today it made her jealous.

Her brother released his wife's arm, and when he turned to Maggie his smile fell away. "Sumner didn't just move here and open a store. He moved in, intending to take my customers and put me out of business. He'll climb over anyone and everyone to get what he wants. I'll admit he's not unique in that way, but is that the kind of man you want?"

Maggie took a step backwards. "I didn't say I wanted him."

"Your eyes say it."

She shook her head, frantic to deny the truth because she knew it would hurt her brother if he thought she was in love with Gordon Sumner. "I would never marry someone who could harm you. I'm just saying he's not as bad as you think. He is competitive, yes, but he's got a big heart. He's been paying Anna Smith higher wages ever since her Pa died. And he came up with this idea for the parade as a way to collect gifts for the orphans."

Maggie tore away from David's steady gaze, crossing to the front window. Snow no longer fell, and people were getting out. Soon, the sleigh would arrive and she would have to put on a happy face and pretend to be Sum's wife. Rather, Mr. Santa's bride.

If only make-believe could be true.

She knew Sum wasn't perfect, and he wasn't right for her, but that didn't stop her from wanting him. He'd been good to her, and his flirting and teasing had been good for her. She'd forgotten what it felt like to have fun. She wrapped her arms around herself, wishing they were his arms. "I don't remember playing much as a girl. He teases me and makes everything we do together fun."

David's voice came from behind her. "Sis, I'm glad he can make you smile. But you know he got you into that parade for his own reasons. It'll give him fine publicity, and he managed to work it out so he doesn't have to spend much of anything to look good."

Her brother's hands came to rest on her shoulders, for the first time feeling heavy, burdensome. "Take care, *Maggeen*."

Her throat tightened at the childhood term of endearment. She didn't recall her father using it, but David did. He'd been ten when their parents died in that terrible fire, old enough to remember. All she recalled was her mother's scent, rosewater, and her father's thick Irish brogue. No photographs survived. Folks said David looked like his father. She also had their father's dark coloring and wry sense of humor. The only inheritance from her mother, as far as she could see, was the watch pinned close to her heart.

"What do you suppose Ma and Da would've advised?" she asked without turning around.

David remained silent for a moment, perhaps thinking. He wasn't spontaneous, like Sum. Her brother reflected before he spoke or acted, especially if it concerned something important.

"They would've told you to listen to your heart."

Chapter Eight

The day turned out perfect for a parade. The snow ceased early, temperatures rose to above freezing and the clouds cleared, making way for the sun. Sum didn't look up at the blue sky, else he would be reminded of something Maggie had said. Then he would start thinking he still had a chance to win her.

Dressed as St. Nick, he guided two white horses, having to explain to children who asked that reindeer weren't native to Kansas. Santa's *sleigh* was actually a wagon with decorative wooden panels nailed to the sides, painted to make it look like it had runners rather than wheels. An actual sleigh would've been ruined if taken over trolley tracks.

Mrs. Claus sat beside him, being generous with candy and smiles. The rich red velvet he'd selected for her dress complemented her creamy skin and dark hair, which she'd attempted to turn gray with powder. She hadn't needed to add a thing to her naturally rosy cheeks.

He'd opted for a simpler garment, a heavy green robe cinched at the waist with rope. Fur trim would've been nice had it been more affordable. Completing the outfit, a wig and a chest-length white beard secured with string hidden by a nightcap.

Maggie looked adorable. He looked like an imposter with fake whiskers.

Sum glanced over again, unable to keep hope at bay. She might've at least smiled at him. Even a friendly look would be nice. She'd smiled and waved at everyone else. He'd done his duty with frequent *ho-ho-hos*, and refused to let on how much her disregard bothered him.

The parade wound through the main part of town, down Wall Street and along the National Cemetery Road. The festive entourage featured numerous decorated manger scenes on flatbeds, as well as children dressed up as angels and elves. Someone had gotten the idea of rounding up dogs and having them haul a cart driven by a lad dressed up as Christmas Past. Sum didn't remember the dogs or carts from the Dickens tale.

After three agonizing hours, the parade drew to an end, the last stop being the street where his store and O'Brien's were located.

"Look, Victoria is waving us over." Maggie pointed in the direction of her brother's store. "She promised me she would muster an army to help with the toy collection."

"I see Mr. O'Brien and your landlord, Mr. O'Connor. Would that be her army, or just the generals?"

Maggie's lips inched up, a slight smile. He could do better.

He made for the hitching post, guiding the horses around a mob of children. "The troops appear to be swarming the streets. Do you think she meant to recruit dwarves?"

That should've elicited a laugh, at the very least an eye roll.

A wiser man would give up his pursuit, but he didn't

know how to quit. Never had. Facing bullies as a kid, and later as a young man, he'd been beaten to a bloody pulp. Chasing his dream of having a successful store, he'd lost his shirt, his home, been threatened and forced to flee, and still he hadn't given up. Once he set his mind to something, nothing stopped him—and he'd set his mind on having Maggie.

"Do you see any toys on the sidewalk?" She sounded worried.

"No, but I left instructions with Miss Smith for all donations to be brought inside in case of bad weather. Maybe your brother did the same. We can check as soon as we get rid of the rest of this candy."

Despite their falling out, Maggie still had some measure of faith in him. He would not disappoint her. If there weren't enough gifts to go around, he would find a way to provide them, even if he had to delay repaying his debts. He could move shells around for another month, and pray no collectors showed up on his doorstep.

After all the gifts were collected, he would help her distribute them. Along the way, he could coax a genuine smile out of her, and if he was lucky, perhaps a kiss. Proposing so soon hadn't been smart. Now he'd have to start over—once he got her attention.

As the wagon rolled to a stop, the army converged, tiny soldiers screaming at the top of their lungs. "Santa! Candy!"

Sum had to scurry to prevent the frantic midgets from overrunning the wagon before he could reach the back and retrieve the candy. Hiking up the long robe, he stepped down, and then hoisted Maggie to the pavement, holding her close, lest she be knocked down.

In less than half an hour, they'd distributed the remainder of the candy contained in the large burlap sack. After the happy hoard raced off with their goodies, a boy dashed up, skidded to a stop in front of Sum.

The lad didn't look much past twelve, if even that. Carrot-red hair stuck out every which way and he'd been cursed with an abundance of freckles. He reminded Sum of how he'd looked growing up, when he had been dubbed *scarecrow* by his classmates.

Sum met a pair of worried blue eyes. Fortunately, he'd managed to slip a peppermint cane into his pocket in case a teary-eyed latecomer showed up. "Merry Christmas, young man. You're looking for candy, I presume?"

The boy bobbed his head, eagerly. Looked like he needed clothing more than candy. He didn't have on gloves or a hat. His pale wrists extended beyond the sleeves of a tight coat, his dungarees were patched together, and his big toes poked out of holes in his shoes.

Clearly, he came from a poor family. Sum frowned. Poor or not, he would offer his own hat and shoes before he sent his child out into the cold with his head and feet exposed.

"Felix!" A raw-boned woman in a rough woolen coat and poke bonnet stalked up behind the boy and took hold of him by the ear. "You don't go nowhere lessen I say."

The child winced. "Yes ma'am."

Sum narrowed his eyes at the ill-tempered crow. How would she like it if someone twisted her ear to get her attention? "Madam, go easy on him. Boys forget when they're excited. Here's a piece of candy for your son."

He held out the peppermint stick. The woman snatched it out of his hand.

"He ain't my *son*," she scoffed. "He works at our farm. Him and those lazy young'uns over there." She indicated a group of younger children, equally ill clothed, huddled in the back of a wagon with no cover. "We heard you was collectin' for orphans. Them's orphans. We come to get whatever it is you're givin' out."

Cruel *and* greedy. Her name went on the naughty list.

"A lump of coal, is that what you had in mind?" Sum inquired.

She squinted with a look of interest. "You givin' out coal?"

Stupid woman.

Maggie came around from the back of the makeshift sleigh, looking none too happy. "Mrs. Meaney, those children are freezing. Get them out of the cold, somewhere warm."

Not even the cavalry could break through the crowd in front of O'Brien's general store. Not to mention, that place wasn't what one might call *warm*. Sum gestured across the street. "Take them over to my store. You can wait there until we sort through the gifts."

The harpy planted her hands on her hips and glared at him. "Jist who do you think you are, orderin' me around?"

"I am Santa." As if he had to tell her. She didn't appear to be blind. "And this is Mrs. Claus. She's in charge of distributing the gifts. No one gets anything without going through her first."

The woman harrumphed. "Well, we better get *somethin'* after coming all the way to town."

She grabbed the boy's arm and nearly yanked it out of its socket when she turned on her heel to leave. The bank president chose that moment to stroll over. Mrs. Meaney elbowed him aside. Looking bewildered at her rudeness, Charlie Goodlander nevertheless tipped his hat.

"Madam, Merry Christmas."

She didn't give him a moment's notice but kept on in a beeline for her wagon.

He replaced his bowler, an amused grin pushed out graying muttonchops on his generous jowls. "Good heavens. Who was that?"

Maggie's worried gaze followed the orphans as their guardian herded them across the street. "Agnes Meaney. She and her husband run one of the poor farms in the area. Sadly, those children are her charges."

Goodlander's amusement faded.

Sum silently vowed to make certain those youngsters received warm clothing and shoes that fit. "Why would any judge in his right mind put children with someone like her?"

"There are few places orphans can go, if no one steps up to adopt them." Maggie slipped her arm through his. Did she realize what she'd done?

Sum's heartbeat accelerated, an affliction that showed no signs of abating. Anytime she needed to hold onto him, she could. In fact, he wanted her to turn to him, and to depend on him, and—if the stars aligned just right—to fall in love with him.

She released a heavy sigh. "I wish we could take those children somewhere they could be with people who care about them."

"Poor farms aren't the best solution," he acknowledged. Sadly, he didn't have a better one.

Maggie turned her attention to the bank president. "What about that idea you mentioned at the meeting, Mr. Goodland? For a children's home, right here in Fort Scott. Where orphans like those could come to live and get the care they need, and a proper education."

Goodlander rubbed his chin thoughtfully. "You know, I have been thinking about that a great deal since you visited our committee. We'd have to find a good location, and raise enough money, and hire somebody to run it."

Sum latched onto a candidate. Convincing Maggie to move back to Fort Scott would be good for orphans like Felix. Her return would also be good for a certain shopkeeper. He didn't wait for her to volunteer. "Miss

O'Brien would make an excellent headmistress. She's kind and compassionate, devoted to children, and went to a teachers' college. That job's readymade for her.

Maggie didn't leap at the opportunity as he expected. After all, it was her idea, even if she'd been smart enough to convince the bank president he'd thought of it first. Surprisingly, she appeared reluctant. "I already have a job, and I can't leave my students. Not to mention, this home we're talking about doesn't yet exist. It would be premature to hire the staff."

"I grant you, it'll take time to arrange everything, but we can get it done." Goodlander folded his arms over his barrel chest. "When I came out here forty years ago, all I owned was a few carpentry tools. Started work, eventually got me a lumber mill. I lost everything in the big fire and had to rebuild. So I built a hotel, and then started a bank. I've been poor as many times as I've been rich. Life's a struggle, Miss O'Brien. Succeeding at anything worth doing takes persistence."

"You know that, don't you," Sum said to Maggie. "And you're as hardheaded as I am."

She glanced upward and a wry smile reappeared. "Why, you flatter me, sir."

"He's right, though." Goodlander grinned. "That's what it takes to make something like this happen, mule-headed do-gooders."

"Mule-headed, eh?" Sum murmured. It fit. No one had ever called him a do-gooder, but there was always a first time. Besides, Maggie had enough good to make up for his bad. "You'd be a compelling spokesperson for a children's home, Miss O'Brien."

"What about you, Mr. Sumner? A sharp businessman like yourself should have some idea about how to raise the necessary funds."

He hesitated, caught off guard by her maneuver. He couldn't come up with enough money to pay his debts, much less start a children's home. "I have a feeling you're the sharper of the two of us. Are you sure I'm the right person?"

The objection died on his lips when Maggie gave him a look that said she expected him to say as much. She saw through him enough to realize he wasn't the charitable soul he'd pretended to be all day. He couldn't expect to gain her admiration if he didn't show some courage.

"Then again, Santa ought to be able to come up with something, eh?"

Goodlander slapped him on the back. "Excellent! I knew I could count on you."

Maggie's surprised gaze told him he'd been correct about her low opinion of him, which her brother, no doubt, took every opportunity to reinforce.

Sum resented not being in a position to refute the slurs. In good conscience, he couldn't recommend himself to Maggie, so he ought to politely back down and honor her wishes to be left alone. His conscience, however, had minimal influence over his desires. If he could figure out a way to win her, he would do it.

Goodlander turned to Maggie with a ready smile. "And you, Miss O'Brien? What do you say? Will you assist me with this project?"

"I'd be happy to speak out in support of a local children's home."

"Not just speak out, you must consider coming back to run it."

The old gentleman's tenacity impressed Sum. Joining forces, they might just succeed in convincing Maggie to return.

"If you believe I could do a good job, I'd consider it." She fiddled with the watch pinned to her bodice, nervous about something, perhaps the idea of being in the same town with him.

"Miss O'Brien, you are capable of anything you decide to pursue," Sum stated. That included marrying her brother's competitor, but he didn't point this out. She would come around only after he proved he was a worthy suitor, which meant taking care of Maggie's orphans.

She craned her neck to peer over at her brother's store. "Oh, I think David and Mr. O'Connor are collecting gifts now. I should go help them and see what we have so far.

Before releasing her arm, Sum reminded her. "You'll come by later. We can talk about our plans for fundraising, and tomorrow we'll distribute the gifts we collected."

He could break through her resistance if he could get her alone.

Maggie pulled free and shook her head. "David offered his assistance. He'll escort me, you needn't leave your store."

Sum was tired of O'Brien inserting himself between them, or was this Maggie's doing? She might be using her brother as a convenient excuse to avoid him. Granted, he ought to be working in his store, making all the money he could make over the next few days. But he also wanted time alone with Maggie. How else would he convince her to give him another chance?

"There's an extra clerk I can call in to help Miss Smith at the store. We agreed Santa would visit the orphans. I'm Santa this year, therefore, I'll be the one to accompany you."

Chapter Nine

Maggie arrived at the Five Cent Store shortly after dawn, just as Sum finished loading the gifts collected at his store. He drew a tarp over the items and secured the sides. Last night, she and David had brought by the items they'd collected. Sum hadn't been happy about that. He'd expected her to come alone. He wouldn't be any happier today when he discovered she had invited a friend along.

What else could she do? He'd been insistent, rightfully so, that Santa must deliver the gifts, but she couldn't risk being caught alone with him. Plus, she had promised to help him find a suitable wife. Her friend also needed a nudge in the direction of the altar, so she'd be doing both of them a favor, even if she didn't feel too good about it.

Throughout the parade, Sum had glanced at her longingly, and tried to joke with her. More than anything, she wanted to enjoy his company, but she sensed he was still intent on wooing her, so she'd turned a cold shoulder—and ended up being miserable, despite smiling until her face hurt. Once he turned his charm on someone else, she would get over this regrettable fascination. She hoped.

"Three poor farms, plus the orphans at the home for the destitute." She checked her list and worriedly eyed the canvas hump. "I hope we have enough gifts. I hadn't received the names of all the children Mrs. Meaney brought to town."

Sum patted the tarp and smiled. "We've got everything they asked for, and that's after I gave Felix and the girls new clothes and shoes."

"You did?" Maggie fought the urge to hug him. That would only encourage him. But she wouldn't pretend indifference to his generosity. "Oh, Sum, I'm so glad to hear it. Those poor children were in rags."

"And I told the old witch I was good friends with the judge and would be sure to tell him how the children were faring."

"You know Judge Chambers?"

"No, but I thought if I told her I did, she'd be more inclined to take care of those kids. I do plan to check on them. If it looks like she's abusing them, I will get to know that judge and insist he find a better place for those children."

Maggie smiled up at him, impressed. "You're so sly…in a good way"

"I'll take that as a compliment." Sum pulled her wool scarf up to the bottom of her chin as if he was afraid she might take a chill. His consideration warmed her more than the scarf.

After he assisted her into the wagon, Maggie adjusted her skirts, mulling over David's warning regarding Sum's self-serving intentions. What he'd done for those children couldn't gain him anything. He had done it out of the goodness of his heart. Although it wouldn't matter to her whether he was self-serving or not, she was glad she'd seen evidence to the contrary.

A single snowflake dropped a cold kiss on her cheek. She looked up, and saw a few more stragglers drifting down from a gray sky. She blinked as one caught on her eyelash. "We better get going so we can deliver as many of these gifts as possible before the snow starts in earnest."

He climbed up onto the seat, adjusted his hat, tugged his gloves tighter and then took up the reins. "If we get caught in a storm, we may have to spend the night in an abandoned barn. Mr. O'Connor told me that's how he met his wife."

"He met her in an abandoned barn?" Unlikely.

"They took shelter after her buggy broke down."

"That sounds very suspicious." Maggie eyed the sturdy wheels and then looked at Sum, askance. "Your wagon appears to be in good shape. You wouldn't purposely strand us."

The devilish gleam in his eyes told her he might.

"Nancy won't like that."

Her remark wiped the smile off his face. "Nancy?"

"I invited Nancy Robinson to come along. She's expressed interest in helping with the fundraising efforts for the children's home. I thought if we brought her along it would give all of us a chance to talk about it."

Maggie fiddled with the drawstring on her purse, unable to look Sum in the eye for fear he'd see what a big fat liar she'd become. She had gone to Nancy and wheedled until she'd gotten her friend to agree to come along under the pretense of being a chaperone.

Sum's cheerfulness abated. The smiles didn't return even after they'd stopped by Nancy's house to pick her up.

He assisted Nancy into the wagon and Maggie scooted over, making room next to Sum. He climbed back up and started out with nary a word. What happened to that chatty fellow who'd talked her ear off on their first outing?

Maggie made light conversation, as best she could with Nancy sniffling. "Are you ill?"

Nancy shook her head. "Just a little sniffle."

Poor thing, her nose had turned red.

Maggie worried that she might've caused her friend to feel obligated about coming along. Thankfully, Nancy had bundled up with a heavy coat, thick scarf and leather gloves over knitted ones. She'd gathered her pretty blond hair into a tight knot and wrapped her head in another scarf before pulling up a fur-lined hood. She looked like an Eskimo. Not ideal situation for an introduction to a potential suitor. If Sum would open his mouth, it might help.

Nancy glanced at him, appearing uncertain as to what to say to a rock. She was sweet and friendly, but not a lively conversationalist. Sum was, and Maggie had counted on him to draw her friend out.

Upon leaving town, they headed southwest along a quiet road. Snow continued to fall in fits and starts.

"What do you make of this weather, Mr. Sumner?" Nancy asked finally.

"If I were in charge of it, I'd make the sun come out."

Nancy nodded, but she didn't pick up the thread he'd dropped.

"Warm weather is so much nicer," Maggie dug behind her for another blanket and wrapped it around her friend's shoulders. "Nancy and her mother own bicycles and they like to go riding when the weather's pleasant. You like bicycles, don't you Mr. Sumner?"

"No reason to dislike them. They don't bite."

"They don't eat hay, either." Maggie enjoyed their banter, but now she had to get Nancy talking. "How nice, you and Mr. Sumner both like bicycles. Perhaps he can join you on a ride."

"Do you ride, Mr. Sumner?" Nancy asked.

"Only if my feet go on strike."

Maggie ignored Sum's attempt to make eye contact. She already knew what he thought of her scheme. Once he got to know Nancy, he would be appreciative of the introduction. "Oh, you should show Mr. Sumner the hair jewelry you make. Nancy weaves hair into different designs. She makes brooches and wall hangings."

"Is that so?" Sum reached up and removed his hat. "What, pray tell, could you do with this, Miss Robinson?"

Nancy eyed his bright hair thoughtfully. She reached up and fingered a strand. "Coarse hair is easier to weave. Yours is very soft, but I could probably do something. I'd need to work with it for a while before I'd know. Is there a particular piece you had in mind?

Maggie bit down on a surge of jealousy. For a split second, she entertained the thought of tossing her friend out of the wagon. She didn't want Nancy touching Sum's hair, or any other part of him for that matter. "I thought most of your jewelry was made as memorial gifts with hair from the deceased. Mr. Sumner isn't dead...yet."

Nancy gaped at her, horrified. Wasn't her fault the nasty remark had just popped out before any real thought could be put to it.

Sum held his lower lip between his teeth and appeared to be fighting a laugh. He returned his hat to its proper place. Redheaded rascal. He'd done that on purpose, knowing it would annoy her. If he imagined making her jealous would stop her from finding him a wife, he was wrong.

Maggie turned to her friend. "I'm sorry, Nancy. You're work is beautiful, and I think a piece with Mr. Sumner's hair would be lovely."

Awareness dawned on her friend's face. Her eyes

twinkled with amusement. "Oh yes, I agree, his hair would make a very striking piece. If you'd like, I'll put it in a brooch for you."

Santa and his helpers delivered gifts to orphans on two poor farms before the weather sent them hurrying back to Fort Scott. Once the snow stopped, they would go out again, tomorrow and then the next day, and with luck, they'd have all the gifts delivered by Christmas Day.

Maggie's orphans would have their presents. Sum intended to ask for one, as well.

The sneaky lass had tried to set him up with her friend, before her absurd attempt backfired. Nancy had spent most of the ride home in animated conversation about all that he and Maggie had in common. He would thank Miss Robinson for her help when he went back to give her a hank of his hair and order that brooch for Maggie.

After returning the sniffling Miss Robinson home, Sum took the wagon back to his store. He hopped down and went to assist Maggie. "I'm feeling charitable. Let's celebrate our first delivery with a cup of cocoa."

She grasped his hand and stepped onto the brick pavement. Instead of accepting his arm, she backed away. "Look at all the shoppers. You'll be distracted, and I need to help David at the store."

With only a few days left before Christmas, scads of people were out, despite the snow, and both stores would be busy, but that wasn't why she wanted to dash off.

"Tonight then..." Sum brushed snow off the sleeve of his dark coat. He'd hardly noticed the cold throughout most of the trip because he'd been having too much fun making Maggie jealous. He'd loved seeing her flush with anger when he invited Nancy to examine his hair. "I'll come by and we'll go somewhere for dinner."

This elicited a look of alarm. "No, I can't possibly. I'm busy…washing my hair."

"Be ready by seven," he said, his optimism undeterred. She'd been ready to throttle her friend for simply touching his hair.

"Sum, I'm not going out with you." As she spoke, a buggy rolled up beside them, driven by Mr. O'Connor's eldest daughter, Phoebe, an independent young woman who enjoyed spending her parents' money in stores all over town.

The tall blonde tied the reins and stepped out, adjusting her fur-trimmed coat over a fashionable cream-colored walking suit. "Merry Christmas, Miss O'Brien," she said, and then turned her bright smile on Sum. "And to you, Mr. Sumner. A very Merry Christmas."

"Merry Christmas, Miss O'Connor." He tipped his hat. "You're looking festive today. I'm glad to see you're willing to brave the snow to shop at my store."

"A little snow won't stop me. You know how I love to shop." She lifted the hem of her skirts, revealing fashionable button-up leather boots, which only proved she wasn't lying about loving to shop. "My boots may be ruined, though. I should've worn galoshes."

"Before you leave, I'll shovel the walk," he promised. "We have hot cocoa inside. Have Miss Smith pour you a cup."

"That sounds wonderful." She flashed another pearly smile. "Do join me if you have time. I need help coming up with ideas for Christmas presents. My parents have everything."

"You might save your money. That would be a nice present." Maggie made the remark dryly, but her face had gotten red again.

The younger woman tipped her head, and to her credit, smiled at the jab. "Yes, that would be a big surprise. Oh, and I meant to tell you, my father will stop by later to deliver presents for the orphans. We had fun picking them out. Spent too much money, I'm afraid."

After firing the sarcastic retort, she tiptoed off through the white powder.

Sum waited until the young woman entered the store, then he couldn't resist. "If you don't go to dinner with me, I could invite Miss O'Connor. She's very entertaining."

Maggie didn't blink. "Her father would shoot you. She's half your age."

His lips inched up. "Hmm. Nineteen times two doesn't equal thirty-two. You need to work on your arithmetic, teacher."

She lifted her chin. "So, you only *look* older."

He wrapped his arms around his chest to keep from laughing. God, she was adorable. He wanted to kiss her, but if he did that out here in front of everyone, she'd never speak to him again.

This was the second round he'd won. However, Maggie wouldn't acknowledge defeat if he didn't give her a way to do so gracefully. "Come to dinner with me tonight and we can discuss more suitable sweethearts. Besides, you owe me for helping you collect all those gifts. I'll consider a night out sufficient repayment."

The tightness around her mouth eased, as did the frown line between her eyebrows. He stepped closer and dusted snow off her cape and hood. Their eyes met, and his heart kicked in his chest. He hoped their children would have her gypsy eyes and midnight hair.

Where had this recent obsession with procreation come from? He'd been with beautiful women before, but none of them had made him long to be domesticated. Never mind. He had stopped fighting this powerful connection—love, or whatever the hell one might call it—and it was time she gave in as well. Tonight, he would make her see that. After he made her his, her love for him would surpass her loyalty to David O'Brien.

He cupped his hands on her shoulders. "Dinner. Tonight. After that, you can send me back to the North Pole if you'd like."

Chapter Ten

At ten minutes until seven, Sum took a final look in the mirror, adjusted his bow tie and smoothed down the points of his collar. He'd put on a black frock coat over a snowy white shirt and tie, and spiced it up with a blue brocade vest. His father, who'd cursed him with tart-red hair, had also possessed a keen eye for complimentary clothing. That one helpful trait, however, didn't make up for the other inferior ones.

He'd also inherited his father's spontaneous nature, which had gotten him into trouble from a young age. That, coupled with a tendency to trust the wrong people, had left him in a financial bind. But if the last few days' receipts were any indication, he would soon climb out of the hole. Once he paid off his creditors, he would start saving for a proper home for his new wife.

Maggie would be his. He'd gain her promise tonight, even if he had to seduce her. Something he looked forward to. He had never set his mind on something that he'd failed, in the end, to acquire. He'd also lost most of what he'd made, but he wouldn't lose Maggie. Her love was too valuable, worth more than all his dreams put together. If she could love him, then he could believe in himself, and he would never be a failure again.

Knocking echoed from below. Had Maggie grown impatient? He could wish.

Sum trotted down the stairs and turned up the gas lever, spilling light into the store. Not seeing anyone at the door, he unlocked it and looked outside, now thinking perhaps it was a childish prank.

A man hiding into the shadows grabbed him by the throat, and putting the cold barrel of a gun to his forehead, shoved him back into the store. His attacker loomed over him, the size of a bull; taller, stronger, and based on the stench rolling off him in waves, fermented in in a barrel of cheap whiskey.

"Don' make a sound, or I'll hafta kill ya." His foul breath wafted into Sum's face.

Sound? He couldn't speak, could hardly swallow past the man's beefy grip.

Debt collector? They were generally unpleasant characters, but this one looked larger and meaner than the ones he'd encountered before.

Sum tried to think over the loud hammering of his heart. Panic rarely helped. "What..." he rasped. "Do you want?"

"Your money. All of it."

So, the bull was a robber, as well as a debt collector. Sum cursed himself for not being more vigilant. Overpowering the massive fellow didn't seem a viable option. He'd fought big men, but not a behemoth that had a gun held to his head. Somehow, he had to convince the inebriated attacker to relax his guard.

"Can't...breathe," Sum choked out.

The sausage-like fingers relaxed their grip, slightly.

Sum swallowed, but was careful not to move quickly and cause alarm. The trigger-happy fool might send a bullet through his brain. "Put the gun down and I'll get the money. It's in the register drawer."

He'd already put the day's earnings in the safe, and there was no way in hell he would hand it over. But he kept a loaded revolver underneath the counter, and if he could get to it...

"Ain't puttin' this gun down 'til I see that money. Let's go over there."

Sum moved backwards, with the man advancing along with him. They inched toward the counter. "When we reach the register, you'll have to release me so I can open it."

That would give him time to knock the man's gun away and retrieve his—he hoped.

Dread tightened a fist around his heart. If he died tonight, he would never see Maggie again, considering they'd end up in different places. Even if she lit a thousand candles, he doubted she could pray him into heaven. Unlike her, he had never been good, yet he yearned to spend his life with a woman who gave him the desire to be better. He wanted to show Maggie how much he loved her every day he was granted life.

Sum focused his attention on the flat-nosed assailant and the gun. He'd watch for his chance and get out of this, just as he'd gotten out of other tight spots.

Maggie checked the watch pinned to her jacket. Ten minutes past. Not once had Sum been late, and now, after browbeating her into going to dinner with him, he made her wait for him.

She paced in the dark store in front of the counter, stopping long enough to pluck a peppermint from a candy jar and pop it into her mouth. The candy would settle her stomach. It hadn't unknotted since she'd left him standing on the sidewalk, relishing his victory.

Arrogant Easterner, showy as a jaybird in his fashionable suits and bow ties with every strand of his gingery hair combed into place, never mind that his smile was downright sinful, and his eyes were as blue as the Kansas sky.

Would serve him right if she went back upstairs. She could spend a pleasant evening with her niece and nephew. They would run her ragged, but that would be more relaxing than staring at Sum over a steak and a glass of wine.

The handsome charmer continued to blast away at her resistance, and the terrible truth was, she actually looked forward to surrender. She'd gone mad since she'd started spending time with him, listening to his blarney. Trying to match him up with her friend, and feeling miserable about it, and then insulting Phoebe O'Connor, who was a very nice young lady, had made one thing clear—she couldn't be Sum's matchmaker. Just the thought of him being with another woman was enough to send her temper soaring.

Crossing over to the front window, Maggie peered across the street at his store. Through an open door, soft light from inside spilled across the snow. She watched for another moment, but Sum didn't come outside. Had he forgotten something and gone back for it? Or had he gotten distracted filling Miss O'Connor's order?

Devil take him...no, she didn't really mean that. She didn't want anyone else to have him, not old Scratch, not Miss O'Connor, not even Michael the Archangel.

David was wrong about what her parents would've advised. If she listened to her selfish heart, she would accept Sum's proposal. Then where would that leave her? Pitted against her brother. Sum didn't understand how this would tear her apart because he hadn't been blessed with a close family. She longed to give him that, and more. If ever there was a man who needed her love, it was Gordon Sumner. But there could be no happiness for them if she had divided loyalties.

She squinted to read his name in shadowed letters on the large glass pane. Why couldn't he have opened a livery or a hotel, anything except a mercantile? If he'd located his store across town, at least he wouldn't be stealing her brother's customers. In spite of it, she still longed to be Mrs. Sumner, Mrs. Maggie O'Brien Sumner.

Her stomach did a slow flip. *O'Brien. Sumner. Together.* Why hadn't she thought of it before? That made perfect sense. Apart, they both struggled, but together, as business partners, they would be unbeatable. Of course, her hardheaded brother would resist partnering with a man he distrusted. Victoria had a more open mind and might be convinced, and then she could bring David around.

The idea gathered steam. Maggie got so excited thinking about the possibilities, she couldn't wait to talk to Sum. If he agreed, they could plan for how best to approach Victoria and David. Although she'd have to give up her teaching job in Kansas City, a worthy project awaited her here, founding a children's home where orphans could be cared for and schooled.

She unlocked the front door. Hugging her cloak, she raced across the street. Gas lamps along the sidewalk illuminated snowflakes twirling in the darkness above the bricked pavement. Her heart danced with them. If she could make a way for her and Sum to be together, it would be the best Christmas ever.

Maggie stepped onto the opposite sidewalk and raced through the open door. She halted, startled by a strange sight over by the register.

A massive, stoop-shouldered man held Sum by the neck and had a gun pointed at his head.

Terror surged through her. "No! Don't shoot!"

At her cry, the huge man whirled around.

She didn't think past her urgency to reach Sum, she didn't think about anything except saving him when she started forward.

The gun flashed fire and smoke, and a loud retort burst in her ears. Something punched her chest. She staggered back, shocked and disbelieving. The blood in her veins turned to ice.

I'm shot. The terrifying thought flickered through her mind, drowned out by a loud roaring in her ears, which grew louder, deafening, even over a furious yell, which she assumed came from Sum. But she couldn't see him. Darkness encroached on her vision.

Her knees buckled, and the last thing she heard was another gunshot.

Chapter Eleven

The bullet whizzed past Sum's head, something on the shelves behind him crashed. He grabbed his revolver from beneath the counter and fired, but the bull lumbered past Maggie's crumpled form and out the door. *The hazy smoke of gunpowder hung in the air and the acrid smell.*

"Maggie!" He rushed to her side, dropping to his knees beside her. His throat closed up like the man's fingers were still around it, and fear compressed his lungs.

She lay sprawled on her back a few feet inside the door. It had happened so fast. She'd appeared out of nowhere, screamed and startled the robber, and the bastard had shot her.

Sum set his gun aside, cursing himself for not being fast enough. He leaned over and gently drew her hair away from her face. "Maggie? Sweetheart?"

Her eyes remained closed, her lashes forming black crescents against pale skin...too pale. Her lips had lost all color. His frantic gaze snapped onto a dark hole burned into her cloak, just left of center above her breast. He sucked in a sharp breath.

"God, no…" He couldn't stop his hands from shaking as he unfastened her cloak. "Maggie…Maggie…." He chanted her name, as if saying it would vanquish the horror and she would open her eyes and smile at him and everything would be all right. His breath came in harsh, painful gasps. His heart felt like it might explode.

"Sum?" Her voice came out small, tremulous, lashes fluttered and a bewildered gaze met his. Relief deflated the balloon inside his chest. If she could talk, that meant it wasn't as bad as he thought.

"Be still." He tried to smile to reassure her. "You'll be all right. Just let me take a look."

Being as gentle as possible, he peeled back the cloak, his gut knotted with fear, anticipating seeing blood soaking her clothes. Her frightened gaze remained on his face as if looking at him gave her courage. For her sake, he would be strong.

The bullet had lodged in the center of the gold watch she kept pinned to her bodice.

He stared in disbelief, released his pent-up terror in a heavy gust. "Thank God."

"How…how bad is it?" She struggled to get up on her elbows, bending her neck to look.

"You're all right, sweetheart." He gathered her in his arms, cradling her close, giddy with relief, almost laughing. The shock from being shot must've caused her to swoon. "You're not hurt. The watch stopped the bullet."

"My mother's watch?" Her anxiousness seemed to increase as she reached for the broken piece of jewelry and fumbled, trying to unpin it.

"Here, let me…" Removing the watch from the pin, he handed it to her.

She stared at the ruined timepiece, her expression turning to disbelief. Tears trickled down her cheeks.

Delayed reaction, perhaps. Gratitude. God knows he wanted to kiss the thing, preserve it as a relic, a miracle.

He fished a fresh handkerchief from his vest pocket. She shook her head when he tried to give it to her. "I already have one of yours, thank you."

"Do you have it with you?"

She sniffed. "No."

"Then take this one and you'll have two." He gently dried the tears from her cheeks and tucked the handkerchief into her hand.

She reached for the bonnet, which had been knocked askew when she fell. He helped her straighten it. Their eyes met and he saw his unspeakable fear reflected in her gaze. She turned into him and put her arms around his neck, clinging to him. "You-you're all right?"

"I'm fine—" The words backed up in his throat. He hugged her close, vowing he would never again let anyone hurt her. He'd make sure she stayed safe, even if it killed him.

Gunshots came from outside, in rapid succession.

Sum tightened his hold instinctively, and reached for his revolver. The gunfire wasn't too distant, maybe just down the street. The bull hadn't gone far, and now he was causing further mayhem. No one could rest easy until the animal had been put down.

"Come on, let's get you somewhere safe." He tucked the gun into his waistband, and then pulled Maggie into a sitting position and helped her to her feet. She still looked dazed.

He pressed a kiss to her forehead. "Upstairs, you'll be safe there while I check things out. Lock the door behind me."

Thundering steps sounded outside on the walkway.

Alarmed, Sum thrust Maggie behind him and drew his gun.

Her brother burst into the store.

"Don't shoot!" Before Sum could lower his gun, Maggie stepped between them.

His heart slammed to a stop, at the same time O'Brien jerked to a halt, eyes wide with surprise. Releasing a furious breath, Sum lowered the gun, and reached for her. "Damn it, Maggie! Stop putting yourself in harm's way."

Her brother's gaze moved between them, confused. "Did you hear the gunshots? Mr. O'Connor came by, and some idiot dragged him off his horse and tried to kill him. I've never seen O'Connor use that gun he wears all the time. By God, he's a crack shot, hit the madman right between the eyes when he charged..." O'Brien's voice trailed off as he approached his sister. "Maggie, what's wrong? Why are you crying?"

"The man he killed is the same one who tried to rob me, I suspect," Sum hoped the bastard roasted in hell. "He shot Maggie. Her watch saved her."

"Shot? Watch?" Her brother honed in on the hole torn in her cloak. Not surprisingly, he reacted with horror. "My God, Maggie. Are you all right?"

Lifting her hand, she opened her palm and showed him the ruined jewelry. "I'm sorry, Davy. The bullet, it-it broke Ma's watch. That's all we had left, and I...I..." The tears began to flow again.

So, her initial reaction hadn't been one of gratitude. Sum couldn't grasp her despair over the ruined heirloom. He'd never treasured anything as much as he treasured Maggie, and would give up any object, no matter how precious, to keep her safe.

O'Brien grasped his sister's arm and pulled her into a tight embrace. His quick action jostled the ruined watch and it fell out of her hand, landing with a clunk on the floor. "Don't cry," he murmured, stroking her back as she clung to him, weeping. "Here now, Ma would be glad of it. She saved you, *Mageen*."

His dark gaze shifted. When his eyes met Sum's there was murder in them. "Why didn't you stop him?"

A question Sum had asked himself over and over. He had no answer. No excuse. He bent down and picked up the watch. "Her mother did a better job of it, I'll admit.

Maggie pulled back with a frown on her tear-streaked face. "David, don't get angry with Sum. He didn't have time to do anything. That horrid man had a gun on him when I came in—"

Sum refused to let her defend him. "I should've reacted faster. Had this watch not stopped the bullet, you'd be dead."

With a dark look, O'Brien curled his arm around his sister's shoulders. "Come on, Maggie, we're going home."

She didn't resist when he guided her toward the door. Sum remained where he stood. She twisted around, looking at him with longing in her eyes, as if she expected him to object to her leaving, or maybe she thought he'd follow.

He couldn't do either because she didn't belong to him. Moreover, he shouldn't have put her into danger. His life was a disaster waiting to happen. Even if he could ensure her safety, he shouldn't have reached so high. Maggie was an angel. He didn't deserve an angel.

"Mr. O'Connor went for the sheriff. I imagine he'll want a statement from you," O'Brien said as they neared the threshold. His tone remained accusing, though his condemnation couldn't hold a candle to the curses Sum had already piled on his own head.

Maggie tore away from her brother's protective hold. "It was a robbery, David. Not Mr. Sumner's fault."

She thought so well of him, he hated to disappoint her. He wasn't the man she thought he was, the honorable man he pretended to be. Feeling exposed, Sum folded his arms across his chest, but then he forced them to drop. Confession didn't come easy for someone who'd avoided it for so long, but it was time he came clean.

"No, Maggie, your brother's right to be worried. It's my fault that man was here. I owe money to a creditor back east. He's not a very patient man, nor is he a nice one. He's sent his thugs after me before. I thought if I paid him part of the money, he'd give me time to come up with the rest. Looks like he's tired of waiting. You need to stay away from me. It's not safe."

Disbelief flickered across her face, then sadness and finally disappointment.

Her eyes had been opened, and now she saw the selfish creature she'd allowed to crawl into her heart. Hopefully, she would expel him quickly and get on with her life.

After Maggie's brother took her home, Sum went to find the sheriff and provide his account of the shooting. The dead man had nothing to say for himself.

Mr. O'Connor reported that he didn't have much choice but to the kill the bastard when the other man stole his horse, took a shot at him and tried to run him over. Any jury would agree on self-defense, so the sheriff didn't bother to bring charges. The lawman did question Sum at length after learning the unidentified man might be a debt collector.

Two hours later, Sum returned to his store, numb with fatigue, yet not so numb he couldn't feel the heavy press of emotion. He'd slipped Maggie's ruined watch into his pocket, after showing it to the sheriff, who'd shaken his head in disbelief.

Sum retrieved the watch to look at it again. It broke

his heart to know she mourned the heirloom. He didn't think it could be fixed, but he would ask the jeweler. If not, he would order one that looked just like it. Somehow, he'd pay for it even if he had to sell his own watch. It was the least he could do, although nothing would make up for what had been taken from her.

He removed his coat, rolled up his sleeves and went to work to keep his mind off Maggie. During the exchange of gunfire, two bottles of Dr. Bradfield's Female Remedy lined up on a shelf behind the counter had been shattered. He picked glass shards off the countertop and the floor, and then wiped up the sticky syrup. His shot at the misbegotten cur had sent a bullet into the doorframe. He pried the slug out of the wood and vowed to practice his aim so he wouldn't miss the next time.

After putting things back in order, he went upstairs. His apartment seemed emptier than usual, even though none of the furniture appeared to be missing. The regulator clock on the wall carried on with a rhythmic tick-tock. With nothing to occupy his mind, guilt rushed in.

Maggie had come within a hair's breadth of being killed. He couldn't have lived with that. Had she died, he would've turned his gun on himself. As it was, he might consider suicide as an option. Death would be preferable to living the rest of his life knowing he'd ruined hers.

For some reason, she'd come across the street looking for him. The anguish in her eyes as she left with her brother told him he had finally succeeded in tearing down her defenses. She cared for him, possibly loved him. Or had before he enlightened her to his true nature.

He'd wounded a beautiful soul, might as well have pulled the trigger on the gun that nearly killed her. Sinking onto the sofa, he braced his elbows on his knees and put his head in his hands. His throat ached, his eyes stung, and still, he couldn't cry, even if it might help release pent-up grief, not to mention self-loathing.

He pressed his fingers against his eyes and rubbed. Pity wouldn't help. If he harmed himself, Maggie would feel worse. The best thing would be to sell everything, repay his creditor and go somewhere far away. She'd be hurt, but eventually she would get over it and be better off without him hanging around, making her worry about him putting her brother out of business. More likely, the clever Irishman would put him out of business.

O'Brien had adjusted well to competition. He was a survivor. So was Maggie, even if she didn't see it. She viewed her brother as responsible for what she'd accomplished. O'Brien might've footed the bill, but she had worked hard to reach her dreams. She'd been orphaned at a young age and might've remained dependent on her older brother, but she'd gone on to become a teacher; not only that, she'd taken up a cause and would see it through.

Maggie let nothing stand in her way.

Sum sat back. He stared at his fingers, surprised by the moisture. Tears? That was something new. He couldn't recall the last time he'd cried. It might've been when he was four, the day his father informed him that his two older brothers had perished at Gettysburg. Far as he could recall, he hadn't wept since then.

A noise came from downstairs, sounding like something had fallen.

Sum came to his feet, heart pounding. He reached for the gun he'd set on the side table. He had locked every door and checked twice, as was his habit. That meant someone had broken in, possibly through the back by the sound of it.

Could be the bull hadn't been working alone and this was his partner or another collector. That made the most sense because being robbed twice in one night was about as likely as lightning striking repeatedly in the same place.

Taking care to remain quiet, Sum crept down the stairs leading to the storage area. He strained to see in the darkness. If someone was down there, he didn't want to turn up the lights and make himself an easy target. Plus, he had the advantage of knowing where he'd put everything. As he placed his foot on the next riser and shifted his weight, the wood creaked.

Sum froze.

Scurrying sounds, like the fast movement of feet, came from the back. A window had been pried open, though it didn't look like the space was large enough to allow a man to crawl through, unless he was a small man. Whoever the intruder happened to be, it sounded like he was on the other side of that stack of boxes containing shoes. He'd be expecting someone at the base of the stairs.

Sum leapt over the railing and landed on the floor with a thud, then shoved the boxes on top of the cockroach crouched behind them.

"Ow!"

The voice sounded young. Whoever it was, he was buried beneath shoeboxes.

Sum slid the gas lever upwards. Light glowed from a lamp mounted to the crossbeams above his head. He cocked the hammer on his revolver. "Come out of there, and keep your hands where I can see them. I've got a gun and won't hesitate to shoot your sorry ass."

The boxes shifted, a narrow hand appeared, and then another one, and then a shock of bright red hair.

"Sonofabitch," Sum muttered. He eased the hammer down and stuck the gun in the back of his waistband before he latched onto a skinny wrist and hauled the intruder to his feet. "Stupid kid, what the hell are you doing? I almost shot you."

Felix trembled so hard Sum could feel the vibrations quivering up his arm. The boy was so scared he might've wet his oversized dungarees. Smelled bad, too. A wonder the stink hadn't reached the apartment before the sounds.

Sum released the boy's bony wrist. No point frightening him to death. He already looked like death warmed over, with no coat, no gloves, no hat, and...someone else's boots, at least two sizes too large. Surprising, he hadn't made more much noise tromping around.

"Where are the shoes I gave you," Sum demanded.

Felix wrapped his arms around his chest and hung his head. Maybe that's why he'd broken in here, to steal more shoes. It was possible someone might've stolen his.

Sum modulated his voice to a calmer level. "Did you lose them?"

The boy shook his head.

"What then?"

"Gave em away."

Well, hell... Sum heaved a frustrated sigh. "I'm not really Santa, you now. I don't have a workshop and don't know of any elves that make shoes, which means I can't afford to keep giving them away."

Felix raised his head. He met Sum's gaze with a challenging look. "Boxer needs shoes more than me. I know you ain't Santa, but you still got lotsa shoes."

"Who the hell is Boxer?"

"My little brother. His real name's Harold, but we call him Boxer because he likes to climb into boxes and hide."

Sum tried to ignore the tug on his heart. For all he knew, the kid was making this up. "And what about the clothes? You give those to Boxer, too?"

"Gave him the coat. Gave the shirt and trousers to

Elsie, so she can wear them under her dress and keep warm."

Sum rolled down his sleeves, chagrined by what he was hearing. "How did we miss Boxer and Elsie the other day?"

"Mrs. Meaney didn't bring us all. She knows if she brings Elsie and Boxer and me into town together, I'll take them and run away. She keeps them locked up in the house most of the time. I sleep in the barn." Felix scratched underneath his arm.

Sum eyed the raggedy child. There were dark circles under his eyes and his cheeks looked gaunt, as if he hadn't eaten in a while. "How did you get into town?"

"Waited until Mr. Meaney headed for town then crawled into the back of the wagon. He's deaf in one ear, so he don't hear so well. He can't see real good, either."

"The four girls I met, are they related to you?"

"No, they're from other families."

"How many children are out there on the farm?"

"Eight of us, if you count the baby." Felix reached behind his neck, going for another itch.

"Someone gave that old witch a baby?" Sum declared, astonished. "That's worse than giving *me* an infant."

A reluctant smile pulled at the boy's lips. "Tommy's Ma was an Indian and nobody else wanted him. One of the older girls takes care of him. Mrs. Meaney will put him to work soon as he can walk. She says white folks can make slaves outta Indians. It ain't against the law."

"The hell it ain't." Sum clamped his teeth shut. He was starting to sound like Felix. "I'll talk to the judge about this. He'll take you and the other children away from the Meaneys."

Felix pawed at his chest. "No room on the other poor farms, that's what I hear; and you can't make us go to that destitute house. It's worse than putting up with mean old Mrs. Meaney." He looked around and scratched his head. Possibly he had lice. He didn't look, or smell as though he bathed regularly. "Could we come here? I'd work for you, and Elsie can cook. Boxer's only seven, but he can help out with odd jobs."

Sum shook his head. The very idea of taking on three children was absurd. He wasn't even married, not to mention he had terrible parenting skills, having learned from two of the worst. "That isn't possible. I won't be around much longer."

Felix looked surprised. "Where you going?"

"Haven't decided."

"Is Mrs. Claus going with you?"

The dull pain centered in Sum's chest began to throb. If only he could take her with him. Once he paid off his debt, they wouldn't have to worry about his creditor sending thugs after them. Wishful thinking. He would never ask her to leave her family behind, knowing how important they were to her. "No, she won't be going."

Felix scratched behind his ear. His scratching was making Sum itch.

"How long since you've had a bath?"

The boy shrugged, making it clear bathing was unimportant to him.

"How about since you've eaten?"

His eyes lit up at the mention of food. "I could eat something, if you're offering."

Sum couldn't throw the kid out. Maybe a month ago he would've, but not after meeting Maggie and learning about the plight of orphans. He also couldn't turn his back on the situation the children faced on that poor farm. With Christmas two days away, it was unlikely a new home could be located, although he would talk to His Honor first thing in the morning.

He would ask the judge to put the three siblings with him until their case could be heard. He had an extra bedroom for the girl and could make a pallet in his room for the two boys. It would only be for a few weeks at most, until someone else took them. In the meantime, he'd start looking for potential buyers for his inventory. Maybe O'Brien.

Sum motioned to Felix. "Come on, then. But you have to take a bath if you expect to sleep upstairs. Don't want the place infested with...with whatever it is you're scratching."

Chapter Twelve

The doctor ordered Maggie to remain in bed after what he called *a terrible shock* to her system. He pronounced she could succumb to illness if she didn't rest and remain quiet. A bruise above her left breast appeared to be the only injury, as far as she could tell. She still got nauseous when she thought about how close she'd come to dying, but she wasn't so weak she needed to remain abed through Christmas Eve, especially given Sum's surprising revelation.

He had some nerve telling her to stay away from him. After hounding her for weeks and finally wearing her down, he thought he could send her away with the snap of his fingers? It would take more than an unprincipled creditor to frighten her off.

She selected her favorite striped suit, which reminded her of candy canes, and paired it with a white shirtwaist fastened with tiny buttons. The collar had a nice bow. She sat down at the dressing table in Fannie's room and took extra care arranging her hair. It took over an hour to pin up the heavy tresses and make the style appear casual. A figured bonnet completed the look.

Gazing at her reflection in the mirror, she touched the spot on her chest where the gold watch would've been pinned and tears gathered in her eyes. That watch was all she had left of her mother. Perhaps the works could be rebuilt, or if not, she would still wear it. The imbedded bullet would serve to remind her that her mother had a hand in saving her life, not once but twice. Ma had been the one to tell Da to put her and David out on the porch roof to get them away from the smoke while their parents tried to find another way out.

Maggie crossed to her suitcase and took out the jacket she'd been wearing, and then recalled she'd removed the watch. Only the pin remained. Perhaps she'd given the ruined watch to David.

Making her way downstairs through the storeroom, she heard the children before she saw them. Fannie and Patrick were playing at a small table near the back, one David had set up, which had toys they were allowed to touch.

Victoria, wearing a white apron over a festive green dress, appeared to be assisting an elderly man in selecting a nightgown for his wife. She must've insisted on David wearing that plaid waistcoat. He wouldn't have picked it out. He waited on another customer while four others stood in line, their arms filled with last minute shopping.

The potbellied stove in the center of the store radiated warmth, and the air smelled wonderful: baked goods, fermented cider, chocolate, pickles, leather and tobacco. She and David used to guess which new items their parents stocked going by smell alone. Funny, how she remembered that but couldn't call her Ma's face to mind.

When the elderly man joined the others waiting to pay, Victoria headed in Maggie's direction. Her frown made it clear she wasn't pleased to see her sister-in-law up and dressed. "What are you doing out of bed?"

"Coming to see my family." Maggie smiled sweetly. She was just as stubborn as her brother's wife. "I wanted to know if you had any luck convincing David to partner with Sum. It makes so much sense."

"For Mr. Sumner, I imagine it does."

Victoria's droll tone grated on Maggie's nerves. "You don't agree it's a good idea? How can you not? We've always known both stores can't continue to thrive across the street from each other, carrying the same goods. David nearly went under two years ago, before you came along and showed him that he was resisting progress for no good reason. He's good at operations and finance, but Sum is a natural salesman. He could sell tea to a Chinaman. Can you not see how well they could work together?"

"I'm not saying it's a bad idea." Victoria laid a hand on Maggie's shoulder, speaking low.

Maggie toned down the volume. David had heard her outburst, if that frown was any indication. She would get nowhere by airing their disagreement in public. "Then why do you say it's only beneficial to Mr. Sumner?" she whispered. "I believe David would benefit from Sum's expertise."

"If he's such an expert, how did he get into debt?"

"I'll be asking him that, but it doesn't mean David shouldn't consider a partnership, or at least be open to talking about it. You'll help me convince him, won't you?"

"Mama!" Patrick tugged on Victoria's skirt. "Kee!"

Victoria lifted the toddler onto her hip. He'd soon be too big for his mother to lug around. "We'll go see the kitty in a moment, sweetie. Let me finish talking to Aunt Maggie. You go play with the train Dada gave you."

She set him down and he toddled off in the direction of a table stacked with glassware. Fannie intercepted him and guided him back to their toys.

"She's good with him," Maggie observed.

"Oh, yes. Without Fannie's attentiveness, we'd have a lot more broken dishes."

"Fannie adores her little brother, and she adores you, too."

Victoria's eyes grew bright. She withdrew a handkerchief from her apron pocket. "Now you...look, you've made me cry."

The former Boston socialite, who'd come to town with no housekeeping skills and little knowledge about children, had turned out to be a wonderful mother. She loved her stepdaughter as deeply as if she'd borne the child. Fannie hadn't spoken for two years after her mother had abandoned her and her father. Then Victoria had come along, and had taught her sign language so she could communicate without words, and had eventually won Fannie's trust. When Fannie had started talking again, it had been Victoria she'd spoken to first.

For being so petite, Victoria had a huge heart. Maggie was counting on it.

She hugged her sister-in-law. "You know I love you as much as if we'd always been sisters."

Victoria returned the hug, and then dabbed at her eyes. "I'll help you convince David without you buttering me up."

"I'm not buttering you up." Maggie smiled. "Well, maybe just a wee bit."

Victoria kissed Maggie's cheek and leaned forward to whisper in her ear. "I'm willing to help you because I know you're in love with Mr. Sumner...and he loves you."

Maggie drew back, now she was the one tearing up. "How do you know?"

"Oh, Maggie. Everyone who knows the two of you is aware of it. Even Nancy mentioned to me that she's anxious to see you and Mr. Sumner wed."

"Nancy?" Maggie's cheeks grew warm. "I tried matching them up."

"Oh, yes, she told me all about it. I wish I could've been there."

Victoria's expression turned from amused to serious. "Mr. Sumner has been by to check on you, but David wouldn't let him upstairs, said it wasn't proper, and Mr. Sumner seemed reluctant to push it. I'll talk to David again about considering a partnership, but you may have to wheedle a proposal out of Mr. Sumner first. Then it'll be harder for your brother to say no."

Or David would get pigheaded about it. The chances were fifty-fifty. But those odds were better than the odds with no proposal. That is, if Sum's offer was still good.

Maggie squared her shoulders. Now that she'd accepted the idea that she was in love with the annoying, charming, pretend Santa, she wasn't letting his guilt or fear stand in the way of their future together. "I'll take care of the proposal. You work on David. He's difficult to turn once he's got the bit in his mouth."

"Put that down!" Sum raced over to where the seven-year-old stood on tiptoe at the edge of the counter, reaching for a bottle of Dr. Bradfield's Regulator.

Startled, the boy twisted, and his heel slipped.

Sum caught the child as he fell, and set him on his feet. His clerk had been with another customer, and he hadn't been paying enough attention. The little imp could've broken his neck, or pulled the shelves down and been crushed beneath them. A wave of fear receded into anger. "What were you doing up there?"

"I asked the child to fetch my medicine." Widow Dobbs stood at the counter, primly looking down her nose.

Boxer set the bottle on the counter. He looked up accusingly through a long fringe of white-blond hair, and then darted around Sum's right side, heading straight for the storeroom. He'd hide in one of the umpteen boxes back there, and it would take hours to find him.

All right, so the boy had been helping a customer, but earlier he'd been helping himself to the fresh doughnuts.

Sum heaved a frustrated sigh. He'd been out of his mind when he'd agreed to take on three children, even just for a couple weeks. The judge hadn't hesitated when he'd asked for them—temporarily. He had assumed some kindly matron who'd raised a pack of her own would be eager to take in three children...until he'd gotten to know them better.

He'd caught Felix sneaking pastries after devouring a huge breakfast. The eleven-year-old had to have two stomachs, like a cow. The boy never stopped eating. Hopefully, Felix wouldn't eat the groceries he was supposed to be delivering. And his nine-year-old sister Elsie knew how to cook all right. Oatmeal. She could make gobs and gobs of oatmeal. Right now, she had her sticky hands all over a shiny glass display top, peering eagerly at bejeweled hair ornaments.

Sum finished filling his customer's order—always medicine, sometimes a black handkerchief or shawl to go with her gloomy wardrobe. She'd become a professional mourner after twenty years of practice. He smiled, ruefully. "Sorry, Mrs. Dobbs. I'm not used to having children underfoot."

"That's obvious," the widow drawled. "You ask me, young man, I think you better get yourself a wife before you start taking in children." With that, she picked up her sack of medicines and tottered away.

The old lady was no sooner out the door than in

waltzed Maggie O'Brien, wearing a candy-striped suit, looking delicious.

Sum's heart slipped faster than Boxer's heel. Sadly, there was no one around to catch it. He straightened his coat and smoothed his hands over the wool fabric. Nervous. Elated.

She approached the counter with a smile that tied his insides into knots. "Merry Christmas, Mr. Sumner."

He fought the urge to drag her over the counter and kiss her silly. Not only would that be ill advised in a store filled with customers, he had sworn to keep his hands off her. It took all his willpower to return nothing more than a polite greeting. "And to you, Miss O'Brien. I trust you're feeling better?"

"I thought I would be." Her smile lost some of its luster. She appeared dangerously close to tears. He couldn't keep up this pretense. He cared too much for her. If he explained why he had to leave, she might not like it, but she would understand and be able to deal with it. Maggie had a deep well of strength. His had about dried up.

"Would you like some cocoa?" He came around from behind the counter and ushered her to the rear of the store, nodding gratefully at his clerk as she moved to take over at the register. "I just made a fresh pot...if the children haven't finished it."

She glanced at him with surprise. "Children?"

He motioned with his head toward Elsie, who had taken a seat and was trying on a pair of ladies' boots while a young woman looked on. He'd asked the girl to assist customers if they needed help. Perhaps she thought that meant trying on clothes for them.

"The Erickson children, all three of them. That's Elsie. She's nine and knows how to cook oatmeal. Her seven-year-old brother Harold, they call him Boxer, is hiding somewhere in the back. He's upset because I yelled at him. He tried to help a customer and almost pulled a shelf down on top of him. Felix, you'll remember meeting him after the parade, is out making deliveries. I've got custody of them until another family can be found. The judge is also looking for a home for three other girls and an infant, so if you know of anyone—"

Maggie placed her fingers over his mouth. Then she lifted up on her toes and replaced her fingers with her lips.

For the love of Pete... Breathing ceased, thoughts stalled. He wrapped his hand around the back of her head, threading his fingers through the heavy curls, and kissed her. Oh God, she tasted wonderful, and he'd been starved for her.

She broke off the kiss much too soon, and slipped onto a stool at the back counter as if nothing had happened, like she hadn't noticed the world tilting on its axis. Patting the stool next to her, she smiled. "You are a dear man, Sum, but you aren't making any sense. Sit here beside me and tell me how you ended up with three children."

He sat. She couldn't have been thinking clearly, to kiss him in full view of everyone in the store. Now, he wasn't thinking clearly, because he couldn't think about anything except kissing her again. But that wasn't why he'd brought her back here. He had to explain why they couldn't be together, after answering her question.

"The Meaneys aren't taking care of the children placed in their charge," he explained. "Felix ran away. I caught him the other night trying to steal shoes. He'd given his new clothes to his brother and sister, and he didn't look like he'd eaten for days. For a fact, he hadn't bathed in a month. The judge said he would look into the situation, and in the meantime, he put the Erickson children with me. It's only for a few days. I'm selling out."

She'd been leaning on the counter, her chin propped on her hand, gazing at him with a look of amusement, until he uttered the last sentence, and then she jerked up straight. "Selling out? What do you mean selling out?"

"If I sell the inventory, I'll have enough to repay my creditor in full, so he won't send more of his goons after me."

"But...you said business had been good this month."

"It has been, but I haven't earned enough to pay off my debt and keep my doors open."

"Why did you borrow so much money from that awful man?" Her chagrin acted like acid on his soul.

Sum rubbed his fingers on the counter, reluctant to tell her how stupid he'd been, but that was already obvious. She'd damn near been killed because of his stupidity. He turned on the stool and straddled the fall of her skirts in order to face her while he told her the bitter truth.

"My father, I told you about him, he was always chasing the next big idea. He'd make money and then lose it, invest and go broke. I wasn't going to be like him, so I put my money into a store and went into business with a partner. We did very well...so well my partner up and vamoosed with all our money. No bank was willing to loan me enough to start over."

Her eyes rounded and sympathy welled in the fathomless depths. "Oh, Sum. That's awful, a man you trusted..."

Sum released a dark laugh. "Yeah, he also happens to be my cousin. I don't have a large family, but the one I do have is worthless. I should've known better."

She grasped his forearm and gave him a reproachful look. "Of course you'd trust your family. I would. That doesn't reflect poorly on you."

"Sure it does." He slid his arm back until he could take her hand and brushed his thumb over smooth, warm skin. So weak, he couldn't resist. Nor could he stop thinking about trailing his fingers over her bare body. "I wasn't careful enough, didn't have money put aside. Just like my father, I invested it all in the business. Couldn't pay my employees, and I burned bridges with suppliers when I didn't pay my bills. I left Philadelphia when the collectors came after me, and I moved onto this corner because I thought it'd be easy pickings."

She gazed at him sadly. Now she knew he was opportunistic, selfish and deceitful. That ought to be enough to warn her away from him.

He let go her hand and plowed his fingers through his hair. He had no business touching her. Only a cad would compromise a lady. "I can't risk staying here and exposing you to danger. Even if I get the loan paid off, there are other people out there who'd take a piece of my hide if they could get it."

Maggie drummed her fingers on the counter. "So, that's why you're treating me like I have poison ivy."

He smiled at her tart reprisal. "Aw, now, it's only been a couple days, and you've been holed up at home. I did come by."

"That's what Victoria told me. The doctor doesn't think I have a strong constitution. He wanted me to stay in bed until tomorrow. That's ridiculous. The only thing bothering me is not seeing you."

Her sweet sentiment soothed his aching heart, although he didn't deserve her care and concern. He took her hand, stroking her slender fingers because he couldn't help himself. "Maggie, sweet Maggie. Don't tempt me. I'm trying to be a gentleman."

She leaned in, her eyes twinkling with mischief. "I don't want you to be a gentleman, Sum. I want you to ask me to marry you and give me another kiss."

Thank God she kept her voice low. He, on the other hand, almost fell off his seat and had to brace his feet on the floor. Ironic, how just two days ago, he'd been plotting to make her fall in love with him, and now that she wanted him, he had to push her away. No, not ironic, it was a miserable shame, and even more so because he'd wooed her, knowing he wasn't worthy of her.

"I shouldn't have gotten involved with you, and your brother is right. You need to stay away from me."

She blinked, looking astonished. "Do I have wax in my ears, or did you just say my brother is right? You've been telling me all along, he has nothing to do with us."

"Yes, well..." He had said that, and still thought her brother had no right to dictate who she married. "The point is, you ought to go back to Kansas City, teach children, and fall in love with a good man."

"Faith. The fairies must've taken my Sum and left a mewling changeling in his place."

"Mewling changeling?" He would've smiled at her colorful choice of words if he weren't so miserable. "For Pete's sake, Maggie. I'm trying to do the right thing for a change. Something unselfish."

She gripped his coat sleeve. "If I wanted someone selfless, I'd marry a priest."

His lips twitched. Lord, how he loved her. She somehow managed to inject humor into even a heated exchange. "Priests can't marry," he pointed out.

Maggie sat back, releasing his arm. She flicked her finger at imaginary lint on her skirt. "Yes, of course I know that, and it's a good thing, too. What with their vows of chastity and all."

Sum swallowed a laugh. "Why are we talking about priests?"

"I don't know. We should be talking about the children."

"The children?"

Maggie cocked her head and gave him a look that said his mind had become slow. "As I've told you before, there aren't many places orphans can go if they aren't taken in by a family. I suspect the only way to find families for the Erickson children will be to split them up."

He didn't like her point, nor did he agree with it. "They can't be split up. You, of all people, ought to know that. They're siblings. All they've got left is each other."

She gave him a pleased smile. "Yes, you're right. That's why you need a wife."

Sum crossed his arms over his chest. She might think she could trip him up by talking in circles, but he was wise to her methods. "A wife? Now, why would I need a wife, when I'll be leaving without the children."

"You can't ensure they won't be split up," she insisted.

"What about your brother? He could take them."

"They don't have room for five children...and Victoria is pregnant again."

There went that idea. "I'm sure someone has room."

Maggie folded her arms in obvious mockery. "If they did, why haven't they taken the children by now? They were orphaned two years ago, and no one stepped up to adopt them. They don't want to be separated, so the judge let them go to the poor farm together."

Sum frowned at her logic. "There's no point arguing. The judge will deal with it."

"He put them with you. I think he knew what he was doing."

"Oh, good grief, Maggie. He only put them with me because I *offered* to take them, temporarily. He's aware of that."

Maggie lowered her arms and her expression softened into something approaching pity. "You know what I think? I think you wouldn't mind if it was more than temporary."

Darned if that didn't feel like a stab to the heart. To be honest, which he wasn't, he had been thinking about settling down and having a family...with Maggie. He hadn't thought they might start out with three children. Wait, they weren't starting out at all.

He huffed, hoping he sounded convincingly disdainful. "The other Sum might not mind, but this one isn't interested in being a daddy."

A loud wail drew his attention.

Sum glanced at the front. Elsie had put the boots away and it appeared she had taken a doll from the shelf over to a little girl, who looked to be about four. The mother glared at Elsie, not appreciating the kind gesture, probably because her spoiled child clutched the doll, crying, and wouldn't be appeased unless it was purchased for her.

"Take that doll away," insisted the frazzled mother. "You shouldn't have brought it over here in the first place."

The woman's churlish tone got under Sum's skin.

Elsie's fair complexion bloomed bright red as she stammered an apology. She tried to take the doll away from the little child, who clung to it and screamed to high heaven.

"Excuse me," Sum said to Maggie. "I'll be back in a moment."

He strode down the aisle between the display cases. When he reached Elsie, he put his arm around her thin shoulders and gave her a reassuring hug. "Thank you for helping out. Why don't you see if Miss Smith might need some assistance?"

The girl's grateful smile turned a key in his heart. He didn't want to admit Maggie was right, because the very idea of taking on three children scared him to death. He would talk to the judge. There had to be a good family out there, somewhere.

The irate mother finally succeeded at wrenching the doll away from her little angel. She hoisted the weeping child into her arms, and turned to him. "Mr. Sumner, you really shouldn't let your children run wild in the store. It's very disruptive."

"Elsie was spreading Christmas cheer. I'm sorry if you find that disruptive."

The woman harrumphed, whirled on her heel and marched out the door. The crying faded, and the store became blessedly quiet.

Maggie came up from behind and put her hand on his shoulder. "Just think, we could give the Erickson children so much more than presents for Christmas. We could give them a home. You are a fine man, Mr. Sumner, and you'll be a very good father."

He reached across his chest and laced their fingers together. Letting go of Maggie and the future he'd dreamed of having with her hurt worse than he'd imagined. He spoke low, so only she could hear him. "Maggie, even if it would be safe for you to be with me, and I'm not convinced it would be, after I pay off what I owe, I won't be able to support a wife or children."

She pressed her cheek against his arm. "I know. That's why you and my brother have to go into business together."

Chapter Thirteen

Christmas Eve had always been Maggie's favorite time of year. She and her brother would go to Mass together, then they would come home and open gifts. Even though they knew what was in the boxes, they still pretended to be surprised. When David had expanded his family, the tradition continued, with the addition of songs and games, thanks to Victoria.

Tonight, however, promised to be the worst Christmas Eve ever because the two men Maggie loved were behaving worse than fractious boys in a schoolyard. David refused to partner with Sum, declaring him to be a financial risk. Sum—stubborn man—refused to consider a partnership because he'd lost everything to a thieving cousin and had vowed never to trust anyone again. Maggie wanted to put them both in separate corners until they agreed to sort out their differences.

Sitting on the sofa, she watched Patrick tear into a box and chortle with glee at the newspaper stuffed inside. He completely missed the toy.

Fannie sat next to her, holding her favorite doll, the

one Victoria had given her shortly after arriving in Fort Scott. The exquisite *Jumeau* doll had been Victoria's salvation because Fannie had immediately grown attached to it, and David had been forced to open his eyes and see that all women weren't like his faithless first wife. He still needed better vision when it came to Sum.

"Aunt Maggie, open your last gift." Fannie set her doll aside to retrieve a beribboned hatbox from beneath the Christmas tree—another compromise David had made for his wife. He hadn't wanted trees, or anything that could catch fire, upstairs. Not after a fire had burned the old store to the ground, killing their parents. Victoria had talked him into putting up a tree two years ago. They didn't light candles, but the tree's branches were covered in decorations, including painted Santa ornaments that David had ordered from New York. Maggie had read about the new electrical lights invented by Mr. Edison, but that wasn't something they could afford.

Fannie plopped the hatbox in Maggie's lap. "It's from me and Patrick."

Patrick didn't move from where he sat tearing up newspaper.

"Oh, I wonder what this could be?" Maggie shook the box near her ear. She didn't expect anything breakable because Victoria had asked her what the children might give her, and being practical, she'd suggested warmer gloves.

She opened the package, removing a nice pair of leather gloves tucked inside, along with a folded piece of paper. When she opened it, Fannie's smile broadened.

"You've drawn me a picture!" Maggie turned the paper to the side. On it, her niece had sketched a crude house complete with pointed roof and odd-shaped windows. Out front, Fannie had placed a few large flowers and a half dozen little stick figures, some with dresses, others with trousers. "What is this Fannie? Is this supposed to be the store?'

"No." Fannie frowned with disapproval. "It's the children's home you told me about. The one you said would be built for the orphans. See them?" She pointed to the stick figures. "They're smiling. They have a place to live."

"Oh, yes, I see now." Maggie's throat thickened. Much as she wished she could help make the home a reality, she couldn't stay without a job, or more importantly, without a husband who could support and help her. Sum had told her he was leaving, and once he was gone, she knew she would never see him again. He was breaking her heart.

Near tears, she hugged Fannie. "Thank you, dearest. I love my gloves and my picture."

David stood and scooped Patrick into his arms. "Time for bed, little man."

Her sister-in-law turned from where she sat at the piano. They'd been singing carols earlier, and Victoria played better than anyone. "I'll take him and change him. Fannie, come along. You need to get to bed, too. Santa won't arrive if you're awake."

Fannie gave Maggie one last hug, and then ran for her room.

Her brother moved to sit beside her. He remained quiet for a moment, perhaps thinking about how to explain, again, his reasons for refusing to consider being in a partnership with Sum; not that it mattered, Sum wouldn't accept a partner.

If neither man budged, she could do nothing except return to Kansas City to classroom. Teaching had been enough for her before she'd recruited Gordon Sumner's help with collecting gifts and he'd showed her the kind of life they could have together. Now he'd taken the dream away. She sighed, slipping deeper into melancholy.

"Will you walk to church with me to light candles?" David asked finally.

This was something they did each holiday, light votive candles and say a prayer for their parents. She had no doubt her folks were in heaven, the prayers more beneficial to those left behind.

Maggie nodded. "Of course. We could've stayed after Mass."

"The children were restless."

True enough. No right-thinking person would allow Patrick near lit candles.

"I'll get my cloak..." She reached for the hatbox. "And wear my new gloves."

David checked his watch as they left the building. Out of habit, she reached inside the cloak for the watch pinned to her bodice, and started. "Did I give you Ma's watch?"

"No. I thought you kept it."

She frowned, trying to remember. "I can't imagine where I would've put it. If Sum had found it, he would've returned it." Even if the watch had been ruined, she didn't want to lose it. She would scour the bedroom and her bags after they returned.

Although it was cold outside, it hadn't started snowing, so the walk wasn't unpleasant. She reminisced about walking with Sum to be fitted for their costumes, when he'd kissed her beneath the mistletoe, and afterwards dragged her down a hill and made snow angels. He could annoy her so thoroughly, and at the same time make her laugh and feel young as a girl. She hadn't wanted to start loving him, and now she didn't know how to stop.

She followed her brother inside the church and over to one of the small side altars, where statues of the saints stood watch over rows of flickering candles with pieces of paper slipped in between. They were petitions from congregants and passersby, anyone who longed for answers, or miracles, or both.

David dropped coins in a donation box and then withdrew a match from his pocket and used a candle that was about to go out to set his match ablaze. She couldn't recall why he did that, but he always did, and then he prayed for that person's intentions as well.

He touched the match to the wicks of two unlit candles. "One for Ma and one for Da, to remember them. We'll pray as they taught us."

Maggie couldn't recall her parents' instruction. David had taught her how to pray, among other things. He'd been more than her big brother. He had been a surrogate father, her anchor.

David had worked hard, scrimped and sacrificed so she could have an education and a better life. Asking him to make Sum his partner fulfilled her dream, not his. She had no right to expect him to share ownership in a business he'd worked hard to build. Then to make him feel guilty for refusing only demonstrated her selfishness. She'd been praying for God to change David's mind, when she ought to be praying for a change of heart.

She pressed her hands together in front of her and bowed her head. It was so hard to trust. God might decide she and Sum shouldn't be together. If so, she had to accept it, and bear the pain. "O, blessed Lord and blessed Mother Mary," she prayed in a low voice. "Accept these burning candles as a sign of our faith and our love for Thee. Please hear our prayers, and also include the intentions of the one whose candle burns low. If it is Your Will, grant our petitions. But above all, cleanse my heart of selfishness and make me loyal and faithful to you, no matter the circumstances or the outcome. Amen."

"Sacred Heart of Jesus, have mercy on us," David added.

After a few minutes of silent reflection, he escorted her outside into the dark.

The wind picked up loose snow from the ground and whirled it around their legs. Streetlights lit their way, the moon hid behind low clouds.

"It's getting colder. The air smells like snow."

"What does snow smell like, *Mageen*?"

She hugged his arm. "It smells clean and bright, Davy. Everybody knows that."

He sniffed the air. "Wood smoke. That's what I smell."

"A cozy fire, and hot cocoa."

"You can smell cocoa?"

"No, but I can almost taste it. Let's hurry back and make some."

As they neared the store, she recognized the man in a long overcoat crossing the street. He held onto the brim of a rounded hat, presumably to keep the wind from taking it away.

Sum halted in front of the steps leading up the outside of the building to the rooms upstairs. He tipped his head. "Merry Christmas, O'Brien. Maggie."

"Merry Christmas, Sumner," David said politely.

Maggie had no idea where Sum might be headed, but she didn't fool herself into believing he'd come over to tell her that he'd decided to stay. He had been firm about his decision.

She fought a wave of anguish and then straightened her shoulders. This must be a test. God wanted to see if she was willing to trust Him. She smiled warmly at the man she loved with all her heart, determined to be thankful for what he meant to her, no matter what happened. "Merry Christmas."

Sum rubbed his arms. "Cold night for a walk."

"We've just been to light candles," David informed him. "Are you on your way to church?"

Sum claimed membership in St. Andrew's Episcopal Church, although he wasn't particularly faithful—two strikes against him in David's book.

"I went to an earlier service this evening." He withdrew something from the outside pocket of his coat. "No need to keep you standing out here in the cold. I just wanted to bring something by. For you, Maggie."

She took the small box, wrapped in pretty paper with a silk ribbon tied in a bow. Her heart fluttered in anticipation. What had he gotten her? Not a ring. "Oh, I didn't expect... I have a gift for you inside. I thought to bring it over tomorrow, along with my gifts for the children."

"They'll be happy to have them," Sum glanced over his shoulder before he replied. "Though I've told them if anything is out of place upon my return, Santa won't be stopping by."

Maggie found his attempts at parenting endearing, if ineffective. "Don't threaten consequences unless you intend to follow through. That's the first thing I learned about dealing with children."

Sum smoothed his mustache, which he did sometimes to hide a smile. "I'd appreciate any wisdom you can spare. Now, I should get back."

No, she didn't want him to leave. Not yet. A miracle could still happen. After all, it was Christmas Eve. "If you can trust them a while longer, you could join us for a cup of cocoa."

She looked up at David, who nodded.

"Yes, come inside," he said brusquely. "Let's get out of this cold."

Sum threw another glance over his shoulder, and when he looked at her, his lips twisted in mock chagrin. "All right. I'll give them a half-hour to wreak havoc."

Chapter Fourteen

Sum followed Maggie upstairs to her brother's apartment. "There's something I need to show you," he whispered near her ear. "The advertisement, I think it's about perfect. I hope you'll agree."

She cast a worried look over her shoulder. "The personal advertisement? Why do you—?"

"Later, I'll explain. First, I need to talk to your brother." He had carefully planned how he would approach her. That is, if O'Brien agreed to his proposal.

He had tried—he really had—to let go of his dream. But giving up wasn't in his nature. He wanted Maggie, and he wanted her more than he wanted anything. Wealth, success, none of it mattered if he couldn't share it with her. But he'd about ruined everything by sending her away and refusing the solution she'd offered. He still couldn't do what she wanted, but he hoped his compromise would earn him another chance.

After taking care of everyone's coats and hats, David O'Brien disappeared into the kitchen with his wife. Those wonderful baked smells filled the air and Sum's nose took notice.

Maggie retrieved a box from beneath the Christmas tree, took a seat on the sofa and patted the cushion. "Sit here, by me."

Her inviting smile did things to him he didn't dare confess.

Sum sank onto the sofa, draped his arm over the back and crossed his leg over his knee. The comfortable furniture, which had been nice at one time, looked worn. Then again, O'Brien didn't have to sell out to pay his debts. Tightfisted, perhaps, but he managed his business well. So well, in fact, he'd expanded. O'Brien could do even better—with his help.

Maggie handed him a flat, decorated box. She placed her gift in her lap, fingering the bow, but didn't untie it. "You want to go first?"

"Open your gift. You can't wait." In fact, neither could he. He hoped she'd be pleased.

"No, I can wait, but I want you to go first."

"As you wish." He ran his hand over the top of the box. "You decorated this?"

"Yes, Christmas cards with snow scenes." She flashed him a mischievous look through her lashes. "I know how much you enjoy the snow."

Sum bit back a laugh. He loved her tart sense of humor, and the fact that she had enjoyed rolling around in the snow as much as he had. "That's true," he murmured. Lifting the box lid revealed a knitted scarf woven with brilliant shades of blue.

"I used woolen thread that matches the color of your eyes," she pointed out.

"Thank goodness you didn't try to match my hair." He lifted the scarf out of the box, and a lump rose in this throat. He couldn't recall getting a gift someone had made to draw attention to his features, to remind them of something about him they found attractive and compelling, and yet, it was so…Maggie.

"It's beautiful. I'll wear it with pride." More than pride, every time he looked at it, or touched the soft weave, he'd be reminded of how much he loved her.

He wrapped the scarf around his neck and gave her a proper kiss on the cheek, which brought on an adorable blush. "Now it's your turn.

She whipped off the ribbon and tore away the paper, eager as a child. That was another thing he loved about her, her childlike curiosity and sense of wonder. Maggie appreciated beauty in all its many forms, and she had a flair for creativity, just look at the pains she'd taken to make a box special. He held his breath as she withdrew the drawstring bag and opened it, and released a relieved sigh when she cried out with pleasure.

"Oh, Sum...my mother's watch!" With a delighted smile, Maggie held it up by a gold chain, the fob that had recently held his watch. He'd buy her a new chain when he had more money.

"The jeweler put new works in it, but he was able to salvage the case." He twirled the watch around. "See? Almost as good as new, just a few scratches."

She clasped the watch tight and threw her arms around his neck, planted a kiss on his cheek, but sat back before he had a chance to embrace her. "You are a dear man, Mr. Sumner. Don't let anyone tell you different."

"That's what I hoped you'd think. My plan must be working."

"What plan is that?" Maggie turned the watch in her hands, lovingly examining it. Her joy with the gift sent his heart soaring.

He would do anything for her, give up everything, that's what he wanted to say—but first he had to make sure he was in the position to ask for another chance. "I'll tell you, but first I have to speak with your brother."

"What is it you want to talk about?" David O'Brien returned from the kitchen. He carried a tray of china cups filled with hot cocoa and his wife followed with a dish of cookies.

O'Brien set the tray on the low table in front of the sofa. "Have some cocoa."

Somehow, he made it sound like an order rather than an offer.

Sum tamped down a surge of doubt. This plan would work, if he could keep his pride in check. He would swallow it whole, if it meant he could spend the rest of his life with Maggie. "I'll pass for now."

He leaned forward, picked up a cup and gave it to Maggie. "Here, you were eager for cocoa, as I recall."

"Yes, thank you." She slipped a slender finger through the delicate handle, rested the cup in her other hand, and took a careful sip. Her gaze searched his and a flicker of anxiety returned.

O'Brien took a cup and found a seat on a cushioned chair. He kept his eye on Sum.

The Irishman didn't trust him, which didn't bode well.

Mrs. O'Brien put the cookies in front of him. He'd swear the smile she gave him was meant to be encouraging. She stood, primly folding her hands in front of her. "I think I'd better go check on the children."

She was making herself scarce. Maybe that smile hadn't meant anything.

Sum knew better than to ask Maggie's brother to take him on as a partner. Hell, *he* wouldn't take him on as a partner, if he were in O'Brien's shoes. No, he had to present a palatable alternative, even if he didn't like the taste of it. "You may have heard I'm selling out."

O'Brien gave a solemn nod. "That's what Maggie told me."

No false sympathy from this one. At least he didn't appear to be gloating.

Sum sat straighter and adjusted his coat. "There's a

proposition I'd like to make. I'll offer you my inventory at a discount if you'll buy all of it, so I can clear my debts."

O'Brien dipped his chin. "Agreed. On the condition, I see what you've got and deem the price fair."

"It will be." Sum knew the value and O'Brien would be getting a deal. "Another thing..." This would be a tougher sell. "I'd like to offer my services."

"Your services?" O'Brien set his cup down, his expression solemn. "What you mean is, you want me to make you a partner."

Sum's mouth twisted in a wry smile. That had been Maggie's idea, and much more than he deserved. "No, I wouldn't ask you to give me part of your business. I'm offering to work for you. My preference would be to start out as a head clerk, but I'll do whatever job you need done."

Beside him, Maggie gasped. He couldn't interpret whether it was a gasp of surprise or dismay. She might not wish to wed a clerk. That was something he'd thought about, but he couldn't come up with any other reasonable plan for remaining in Fort Scott. He could work for another mercantile, But O'Brien had the most successful store in town and would be able to afford a head clerk because the business would double in size. Sum knew how to sell things; he just wasn't very adept at holding onto them.

The rent on the building across the street had been paid through the first six months of the year, which would give him and Maggie, and the three children, a place to live until he could find another place.

O'Brien rubbed his chin, appearing deep in thought. He held Sum's gaze for another uncomfortable moment. "Why would you do this? Why not take out a loan from the bank and pay off the creditor, keep your doors open."

Sum had already told Maggie why that wouldn't

work, but it appeared she hadn't shared his shameful past with her brother. Considerate and trustworthy, two more qualities he loved about her. He'd add those to the list in his pocket. When they'd worked together on the personal advertisement, she'd assigned a number of good traits to him, although her perspective might've changed, now that she knew him better.

Her brother already thought poorly of him, and now he would be adding more to what were too many reasons already. If he managed to pull this off and win Maggie, it would be a miracle.

Sum folded his arms over his chest, for fear his hands would shake. "No self-respecting financier will loan me money once they find out I defaulted on a bank loan in Philadelphia and left without paying my suppliers."

O'Brien's expression remained unreadable as a rock. This confession wouldn't help his cause, Sum knew that already, but he wouldn't enter into an agreement without putting all of his proverbial cards on the table. Honesty and trust had to be the basis of any relationship or it wouldn't work.

"I found a creditor willing to give me enough to open a store out here. He was willing to take the risk in return for a high rate for the use of his money. He's the one I thought sent that thug. As it turns out, the bull who tried to rob me was a wanted criminal. He must've thought my store looked like an easy mark. But, Mr. Sikes has sent collectors after me before, and I've no doubt he'll do it again, which is why I need to repay him as soon as possible."

Taking a deep breath, he rested his hands on either side of him, trying to appear calm but unable to keep from curling his fingers into the sofa cushion. Maggie gripped his hand. He tightened his fingers, holding onto her.

If she let him, he would hold on for the rest of his life. The kind of stable, secure love she offered was something he hadn't experienced and wouldn't have believed in if he hadn't met her. He prayed she wouldn't retreat now that she realized how poor they'd be. If O'Brien turned him down, he would have to rethink his options, which were, admittedly, few.

Maggie clung to Sum's hand. He appeared calm, his lips in a customary half-smile, a wry expression just beneath the surface, but his tight grip on her hand said different. Her heart constricted in sympathy. He had to be dying inside, waiting for David's answer. Sum was a proud man. Yet, he'd set aside his pride and come to his chief competitor with his hat in his hand, begging for a job.

Why?

He loved her. There could be no other reason he'd go to such lengths, save to keep the children. Maybe that was part of it, too. He'd thought about what she'd told him about the possibility they'd be split up and had decided he couldn't entrust their future to someone else. She didn't think it possible to love him more, but she did. Entirely. Completely.

She continued to hold Sum's hand, despite her brother's questioning gaze, letting David know that she could not, would not, let go. Sum needed her and she needed him, and they would find a way to be together, even if David refused to hire the man who would soon be his brother-in-law.

David leaned back, threading his fingers through his wavy, black hair. A sign he found the decision difficult. Why couldn't he just say, *yes?* Sum had agreed to do whatever job David assigned him. He couldn't bow any lower.

The prayer she'd recited earlier nudged her conscience. She'd asked forgiveness for being selfish, but was it selfish to love someone? The Blessed Lord had given everything out of love. Sum had given up his pride and his dreams to be with her.

Now she knew why he wanted to share that letter.

"May I see that advertisement you worked on?"

He appeared uncertain at first, and she thought he might not give it to her. Then, with a wry smile, he reached into a small pocket on his waistcoat and withdrew the folded paper. "I took the opportunity to tweak it."

The edges looked a bit ragged, as if he'd been carrying it around. He'd never posted it, and now he wouldn't have to because she would see that he got the bride he wanted.

She plucked it out of his hand, speaking to her brother. "Sum agreed to let me help him craft an advertisement for a mail-order bride, as he found himself in a need of a wife. You'll remember how well I did with yours. Oh, and by the way, you've never thanked me for Victoria."

David pulled his arms around his chest and arched an eyebrow at her. It appeared he wouldn't be offering his gratitude tonight, either.

Maggie unfolded the paper and smoothed it on her lap. Sum's bold handwriting appeared, above her small, neat script. Indeed, he had altered it, and added a few things. "Let me read you what Sum and I came up with."

"Unattached shopkeeper," she started, and then looked at him with surprise. "You removed successful."

Sum shrugged. Modesty didn't become him. She missed the cock-sure Sum who'd pursued his dreams and her with supreme confidence. He'd be back, just as soon as he got his feet under him again.

"You are successful, you know. Successful in the ways that count."

She started over with her original version. *"Successful shopkeeper in fast-growing Western community seeks educated, attractive young woman with exemplary reputation for purposes of marriage. Applicant must be kind and cheerful, willing to work long days, and will need patience..."* She slid a glance at Sum and smiled, remembering his initial reaction when she'd read it the first time.

His expression remained neutral but his eyes gleamed with amusement *"Will need patience with children...three to start with."*

Just as she'd thought, he meant to keep them, dear man.

"Glossy black hair and gypsy eyes preferred; playful and good-tempered, keen on riding sleds and making snow angels." She swallowed a laugh. *"Will provide a comfortable, safe home and be a loving husband and father; am occasionally humorous, engaging, affectionate and generous. Signed, Santa Claus."*

"Describes you perfectly," she told him, and then she turned to David, who had a tight smile on his face from struggling to not laugh out loud. "I believe I meet this gentleman's requirements. I'm going to respond...and I hope he'll answer."

Sum gazed at her with love shining in his eyes, as well as a hint of mischief. Her life with him would never be dull. He put his arm around her. "No need to wait. I'll answer right now. Will you be my Mrs. Claus?"

"Gladly." She leaned in for a kiss and he obliged her. His lips were firm, smooth and warm, and his mustache tickled. She didn't mind the soft hair above his lip but was glad he didn't have a full, flowing beard.

"I love you," he murmured in between kissing.

"I love you, too." She threaded her fingers through

his thick, burnished hair, and melted against the lush pressure of his lips. His hands moved up her back, sending delicious tremors through her.

"Are you two done yet?" David's pointed remark burst their amorous bubble.

Sum drew back with a half-smile on his lips. "We're just getting started."

"Not here in my parlor."

Maggie knew she had a stupid grin on her face, but she couldn't stop smiling. Sum had proposed. They would be married—although they might not be able to stay in Fort Scott if Sum didn't have a job. That would be all right, they could come back for visits. "If David doesn't hire you, we can live in Kansas City and I'll continue teaching. We'll adopt the children and take them with us."

"Slow down, Maggie." David shifted forward on his chair. He rested his arms on his knees and clasped his hands together. He wasn't smiling, but he wasn't frowning, either. "Give me a chance to say something."

She gripped Sum's hand tighter. "Yes?"

David didn't address her. Instead, he spoke directly to Sum. "Hiring you as a clerk isn't the best option."

Sum took the news without flinching, and didn't even act angry. "Very well, I'll look elsewhere."

David held up his hand. "Hear me out before you do that. I'm of the mind that you should continue to run the Five Cent Store, concentrate on what you do best. Frankly, I'd prefer to focus on hardware and expand the bicycle shop. We can split up the business that way— two stores offering different merchandise under a combined name—and still be responsible for our own operations. We'll take a share of each other's profits. Insofar as your debt is concerned, sell off any excess inventory to whoever will give you the best price, and I'll make up whatever difference remains."

For once, Sum didn't speak right away. Actually, he appeared stunned.

Overjoyed, Maggie leapt up and ran to hug her brother's neck. "Oh, David, thank you. Thank you." He returned her embrace without comment or fanfare, in keeping with his nature, which was to downplay his generosity.

She turned to Sum, smiling. "It's a good idea, don't you think?"

"It's a generous offer." His russet brows drew together. "But I can't take it."

Maggie gaped at him. "You can't take it? What do you mean, you can't take it?"

"I'll not accept charity. If, after I sell my inventory, there's enough money left to do as David suggests, then I'd be happy to go into business with him."

There might not be enough, but she wouldn't embarrass her fiancé by saying so, and she understood his reluctance, yet... "I've invested a little money in Mr. Ford's new company. I'll sell my shares."

Sum's eyebrows jumped. "No. Keep your investment, I hear there's a fortune to be made in Ford's horseless carriages."

David harrumphed. "Those wind-up machines won't replace horses."

"What wind-up machines?" Victoria returned to the parlor from her extended departure. Maggie knew her sister-in-law had left to give them privacy to discuss sensitive matters, and she also suspected Victoria had put some ideas into David's head. He was a smart man, but his wife was every bit as clever.

"The horseless carriage," Maggie explained. "I've invested a small amount of money, but Sum and I will be married, and we may need the extra cash."

"Married?" Victoria's eyes grew wide. She rushed over and threw her arms around Maggie's neck.

"Congratulations, darling. I'm so happy for you! I knew you two would work things out."

"They've worked out their marriage. Now Mr. Sumner needs to decide whether he'll go into business with me," David said.

Sum stood and moved next to Maggie, slipped his arm around her waist. The possessive gesture produced a thrill. "Call me Sum," he said to David. "All my friends do, and seeing as you'll be my brother-in-law—"

"And your partner," Maggie reminded him. "Sum and David are going into business together," she announced to Victoria.

"That's splendid news." Victoria sailed to her husband's side and gave him a quick kiss. He smiled and wrapped his arm around her. She reached up and stroked his hair, lavish in her affection, another endearing quality. "You should announce the new partnership in the newspaper."

Maggie went along with Victoria's gentle prod. "I think that's a marvelous idea."

"First, let's see if I can cover the costs," Sum warned. He hugged her, though, and so reassured her that he wouldn't be backing out on his proposal, even if they ended up having to leave town.

Victoria turned in her husband's arms with a thoughtful expression. "My father recently sent me a small sum of money to invest after I wrote to him about the business opportunities out here. I'd like to invest in your Five Cent Store, Mr. Sumner."

Sum didn't look a bit fooled by her attempt to bankroll him. "If we go into business together, we'll share the profits."

"That's between you and my husband. I'm talking about a separate agreement. My father has never trusted me in business matters before now. You won't let me down, will you?"

Maggie circled her arm around her fiancé's lean waist. "He'll double your money, I'm sure of it."

"Maggie, you can't promise her that," Sum muttered next to her ear.

"You can."

He shook his head, utterly serious. "I'm done with risking so much. My family deserves a more prudent provider."

David, for once, spoke first. "Sum, your risks would've paid off if your partner had been honest. As Victoria will tell you, I'm a stick-in-the-mud. I need someone who will push me to take more risks. We'll balance each other out. And I happen to think my wife is right, you'll double her father's investment."

David walked over and put out his hand. "Let's shake on our new venture. *O'Brien and Sumner.*

If Maggie hadn't been watching Sum's face carefully, she might've missed the flash of emotion David's remarks elicited before the familiar wry smile reappeared. Her beloved hesitated only a moment and then shook David's hand.

"*Sumner and O'Brien* has a better ring, don't you think?"

Epilogue

December 23, 1901, Goodlander Home for Children, Fort Scott, Kansas

"Fear not! We bring good tidings of great joy…" A freckled lad standing in the front of the small-fry choir shouted the verse loud enough to pierce every eardrum in the parlor.

The band of angels that broke into song wouldn't have frightened shepherds, but they were cute as all get out. Their smiling director and teacher, Mrs. Sumner, waved her arms and kept them singing. More importantly, she gave them a reason to sing about miracles. Under her tutelage, The *Goodlander Home for Children* prospered.

Charlie Goodlander leaned back in the folding chair, one of a dozen set up in the front parlor of his father-in-law's former home for the purposes of a Christmas concert. He shifted his substantial weight to relieve a cramp in his back and rested his arms across his chest, grinning at a little girl in a white dress with a pair of

144

wings off-kilter. His knees didn't like sitting this long, but he'd put up with the aches and pains to see the smiles on these kids' faces and to know he'd played a small, but important role in putting them there.

The children's home had opened its doors earlier this year, moving into what had been the old fort's officers' quarters and later the home of pioneer settler Horatio T. Wilson.

Charlie squeezed his Lizzie's soft hand. His wife thought it a wonderful idea to turn her family's former residence into a safe, loving home for orphans and had declared she would consider the children who lived here to be their children, as they hadn't been blessed with any of their own. He was glad he could give her a family, at last.

"Hark the herald angels sing, glory to the newborn King," the children sang. They sounded pretty good, not heavenly, but close.

It had taken darn near ten years to get this dream off the ground, starting with talking Mr. and Mrs. Sumner into being on the board and then convincing them to run the place. They'd moved in earlier this year with their brood: Elsie, a blond beauty of eighteen, Davy, a rambunctious eight-year-old who looked just like his namesake, and six-year-old twins Annabelle and Francis, blue-eyed cherubs with hair red enough to catch fire. Felix Sumner, the oldest adopted boy, now a strapping young man of twenty-one, and his tow-headed sixteen-year-old brother, Harold, had remained in the apartment above their father's store where they worked.

Also living at The Goodlander Home were fifteen orphans, all under the age of ten. Soon, that number would swell to twenty. Mrs. Sumner had a hard time turning children away.

As the last verse came to a close, Charlie clapped loudly along with the others, board members mostly, and the Sumner's large and extended family, which included David and Victoria O'Brien and their clan of six children and one on the way.

"Bravo!" Charlie hefted his heavy frame out of the squeaky chair. Sounded like it might not hold out. Better to stand. He'd hate to end up on the floor on his big ass.

He clapped his good friend, Buck O'Connor, on the back. O'Connor, being a tall fellow, wasn't as fat, but he had whiter hair. "Those kids better be in this year's parade, Mr. Mayor."

"They will be," Buck assured him, with a smiling nod at his wife, who'd gone over to congratulate Mrs. Sumner. "Amy and the girls helped with the costumes."

His daughters were grown with families of their own, but he still called them *girls*.

The big man leaned down and cupped his hand to his mouth, whispering in Charlie's ear. "You better tell her they look nice. I mentioned an irregularity with the wings and about got my head taken off."

Charlie chuckled. "'Course you did, because you had to open your big mouth. I swear Buck, you and Amy enjoy a good dispute better than any married couple I know."

"It's not the dispute we enjoy so much," O'Connor drawled. "It's the making up afterwards."

Charlie couldn't contain a bellow.

"What's got you laughing this time, Mr. Goodlander?" Gordon Sumner's wry smile said he'd like to be in on the joke, whatever it was. He had a sharp sense of humor, as dry as O'Connor's. The two made good drinking buddies.

"Oh, nothing in particular, just O'Connor here. He has a funny-looking face."

Sumner smoothed his hand over a fake white beard, which he'd donned for the event, along with robe and a long cap. Didn't seem to bother him to look ridiculous.

He eyed the Mayor. "Hmm, maybe." Then Sumner turned to Charlie. "Have you checked in the mirror lately?

Charlie gripped the smartass by the shoulder. "No, Santa, I don't look into mirrors. Reminds me why Lizzie turned me down three times."

"Excuse me!" Mrs. Sumner said loud enough to be heard over the conversation. "We'll be serving cookies and cocoa in the dining room."

The parlor cleared of children in a matter of seconds, their excited voices trailing behind.

Mrs. Sumner sallied over, all dolled up in a pretty red dress with a white lace cap. She still had to put powder in her hair to make it look gray. Her dark gaze roved each man in turn, suspicious, but still smiling. "What are you three conspiring about over here?"

"What makes Charlie's face so funny," her husband answered smoothly.

"Methinks it's the muttonchops," O'Connor said with a deadpan expression.

"When they lay me out, will you make sure not to invite these two?" Charlie begged her.

She hugged his neck. "Your face isn't a bit funny-looking, just jolly. In fact, I was telling Sum the other day that you should play Santa in next year's parade."

Charlie's heart darn near gave out. He wouldn't have to don a white beard or wig, already being well grizzled, nor would he need any padding around the middle, but he wasn't about to put on that bathrobe and cap and ride around town in a fake sleigh. He'd never live it down.

"Oh, now, you don't want to sit next to an old man like me."

"I'd be honored." She said it with nary a smile.

He wouldn't do it for anybody else, save maybe Lizzie, who wouldn't have asked him in the first place. But this was Maggie Sumner, the woman who had helped him achieve his dream of leaving a legacy. He couldn't disappoint her. "Why, that's mighty nice of you to ask, Mrs. Sumner. I reckon if I could play Santa in the parade next year, I'd die a happy man."

He'd speak to Lizzie later. She'd help him find some way out of it before next Christmas.

The End

༄

Have you read Victoria's story? ***Victoria, Bride of Kansas*** is 34th in the unprecedented 50-book *American Mail-Order Brides* series. If you enjoyed reading her story, there are 49 more books in the series! Find out about the rest of the *American Mail-Order Brides* at http://bit.ly/NewWesternRomance.

Author's Note

This is the third story I've set in historic Fort Scott, Kansas. I fell in love with this town when I first visited Lyons Twin Mansions, a Victorian B&B. After I toured the Fort Scott National Historic Site, part of the U.S. National Park Service, I became interested in Fort Scott's past and knew I wanted to write historical romances set in this fascinating town.

Her Bodyguard takes place in Fort Scott and surrounding counties, circa 1870, during the early railroad boom. *Victoria, Bride of Kansas*, and *Santa's Mail-Order Bride* are set in the early 1890s, Fort Scott's heyday. All three books feature historic locations, events and even a few colorful pioneers. One of these early residents was Charles W. Goodlander, whose fictionalized character appears in *Her Bodyguard* and *Santa's Mail-Order Bride*.

Charlie, as he liked to be called, was a leading citizen and generous philanthropist. He arrived in Fort Scott as a young man in 1858, the first passenger on the first stagecoach from Kansas City. (He'd later declare he needed his "medicinal" flask for the wild, bumpy ride.) He took up contracting and building, and over the years expanded into other ventures, including a lumber mill, a brickyard, a furniture store and hotels. He made and lost several fortunes, his mill being destroyed by fire and rebuilt twice. He helped organize the Citizens' National Bank as its president and served a few terms as mayor of Fort Scott, but largely steered clear of politics. His career was that of a successful businessman, marked by ability, honesty, integrity and fair dealings with his fellow man. His never-give-up approach to life exemplified the spirit of the men (and women) who settled this town.

In 1901, Goodlander bought from the heirs of Col. H. T. Wilson, his father-in-law, the old Wilson home (previously officers' quarters within the old fort) and converted the large structure into The Goodlander Home for Children. The orphans' home served over 800 children from Fort Scott and the surrounding vicinity until it closed in the early 1960s.

On Dec. 17, 1872, Mr. Goodlander wed Elizabeth Clay, daughter of Col. H. T. Wilson. They had no children. Mr. Goodlander passed from this life on May 22, 1902. To my knowledge, he never played Santa Claus.

*You met Mr. O'Connor, the successful businessman, in Maggie's story. Meet the younger, dangerous outlaw in his own story, **Her Bodyguard**.*

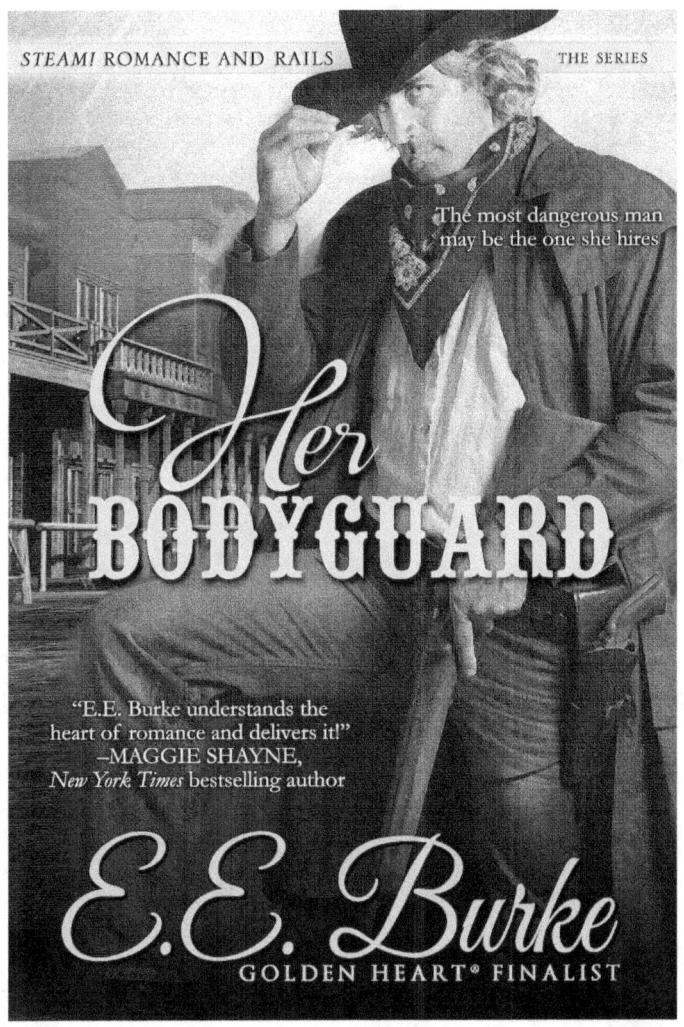

STEAM! ROMANCE AND RAILS

THE SERIES

The most dangerous man
may be the one she hires

Her
BODYGUARD

"E.E. Burke understands the
heart of romance and delivers it!"
–MAGGIE SHAYNE,
New York Times bestselling author

E.E. Burke

GOLDEN HEART® FINALIST

Chapter One

March 1, 1870
Former Cherokee Neutral Lands,
Southeast Kansas

ell must be like this. Not lit with blazing fires, but cold and gray, barren as the dead prairie. Even the wind howled like a deranged demon, flinging bits of ice into Buck's face.

He drew the blanket and oilskin tighter, although nothing warmed the persistent chill in his bones that'd gotten worse as he'd ridden north through Indian Territory. He was a walking dead man here in Kansas, so it seemed somehow fitting he'd entered the abode of the damned.

He patted Goliath's neck, glad for the company of his horse. He had few acquaintances, even fewer friends, and none who would risk their necks for another man's cause. Buck wouldn't have risked getting his neck stretched had the plea not come from his only remaining kinsman. Although at this point, freezing to death seemed more likely than being lynched.

The saddle creaked as he straightened. All around, he could see nothing but mounds of switch grass and stunted trees. No houses or barns, not even smoke from a chimney. He swore, his breath sending out a white cloud. The wind snatched it away. His plan had been to reach Girard before dark, buy a hot meal and a warm bed before meeting with his cousin to get details on the job he'd come to do. But he couldn't risk going on. He had to find shelter.

The fading daylight and worsening sleet made it difficult to see, but was that something just ahead? Buck touched his heels to his stallion's sides, moving closer to the mass taking shape. A buggy, slumped to one side. In front of it stood a single horse with its head down and a woman huddled in a cloak, removing the traces. What the hell was she doing out here all by herself?

Buck sat back in the saddle, uneasy. He'd made it a habit to avoid damsels in distress after being betrayed by one. However, he couldn't very well leave a woman out here on a lonely road in the middle of an ice storm. With a muttered curse, he kicked Goliath into a fast trot.

On his way to her, he passed the buggy's rear wheel, lying on its side in the brush like a wounded animal. Odd, he'd never seen a wheel fly off like that. Generally, the metal rim popped or a spoke snapped. Had the axle nut been loose when she started out? She was damn lucky the buggy hadn't rolled on top of her. He had seen *that* and it wasn't pretty.

His stallion whinnied, excited by the scent of the woman's horse. The mare threw its head and answered.

The lady hadn't noticed him because she was so focused on unhitching the fidgety bay. But now she whirled around. Her hood, drawn low over her face, shadowed her expression but it was clear by her startled response she hadn't expected anyone to come up on her.

Rather than calling out for help, as he anticipated, she dashed toward the buggy's compartment.

The mare shied away from the sudden movement, then reared up, squealing. The buggy started to rock.

"Look out," Buck hollered.

The woman didn't move away from the danger. Instead, she dove into the compartment.

"Goddamn it!" The curse was lost in the wind. He came out of the saddle, dropped the reins on the ground. In a few long strides he'd reached her. "Get out of there."

What the hell was she doing? Trying to crawl beneath the buggy's seat?

The contraption tipped dangerously to one side. Buck snaked an arm around her middle and hauled her out of the death trap.

She twisted around, yowling like an enraged cat. "Get your hands off me."

Her horse squealed and tried to run. The lame buggy hopped.

"Stop screechin'. You're scaring the hors—" Something blistered Buck's cheekbone. "Ouch! What the devil?"

"Let me go!" She went for his face again with her claws.

"Stop that." He swatted her hands away, but managed to keep hold of her while he backed away from the buggy. "I'm just tryin' to—"

Her sharp teeth sank through the leather glove into his finger.

"Blazes!" He yanked his hand away and then grabbed a flailing arm, pinning her against him. Splaying his fingers over the side of her head, he smashed her cheek against his chest to prevent her from biting him again.

Furious screams became muffled growls. Her booted feet, dangling above the ground, lashed out to kick him.

Thank God her skirts got in the way or she would've hammered his shins.

"Stop fighting, you loony woman." He sucked in a breath and checked his temper. Large as he was, and with her no bigger than a minute, he could easily break her.

As he adjusted his hold on her, the hood of her cloak fell back. His fingers slid through a silken mass of hair. In an instant, he became aware of the woman he held—her soft breasts and flaring hips, a delicate fragrance like wildflowers. Something hot and primitive coursed through him. His body responded before his brain could catch up.

She must've sensed his reaction because she started swinging her legs again.

He held her tighter. "Will you *listen?* I'm tryin' to help."

"Not...helping." She gasped the words. "You're...choking me."

Buck eased his hold. His physical reaction couldn't be helped, but he could sure as hell control his strength and keep from hurting her. "All right. I'm setting you down." He hesitated a moment before releasing her. "Don't fly at me with those nails."

She raised her eyes. The black centers swallowed the golden irises like an eclipse of the sun.

His gut clenched. He'd seen that look in the eyes of men he'd faced down, but not women he aided. He hadn't meant to frighten her. He frowned, more comfortable with being annoyed. "That horse about pulled the buggy over on top of you. That's why I grabbed you."

Her dark brows winged up. "You...you were *helping* me?"

"That was the plan."

She seemed further confused when he snatched his

blanket off the ground where it had fallen during their tussle and flung it around her. Then he set off to retrieve her horse. That buggy wasn't going anywhere.

He approached the nervous mare with soft, shushing sounds and laid his hands on its quivering withers. The frightened creature stilled and let him remove the traces.

Sleet peppered the brim of his hat, although the worst of the storm seemed to have passed. He took a look around the bleak surroundings. They were still were in danger of freezing if he didn't find shelter soon.

After unhitching the harness, he brought the horse around. Thankfully, the woman hadn't run off. She'd inched over to the buggy compartment and was rummaging around again, maybe looking for something.

"Unless you've got an axle nut in there, we can't fix this buggy. Can you ride?

She whirled around with a tiny pistol clutched in her hands. "I'm not g-going anywhere with you."

Buck's pulse kicked up a notch. Her hands shook so hard he worried she might actually fire the damn thing before he could talk some sense into her. "You plan on staying here?"

Her chin came up. "I plan on taking *my* horse."

He bit back a curse. Did she think he was *stealing* the nag? Why was he even bothering to help her? He might as well head off down that road, leave her to her own devices. No one could blame him. Only…he'd never abandon a woman. Not even one that was stark raving mad.

"Blast it, I don't have time for this foolishness," he muttered.

He offered her the reins, but when she reached out to take them, he locked his fingers around her wrist and nabbed the gun. Then he hauled the reluctant damsel to where he'd left Goliath.

The stallion had remained, as trained, right where

they'd stopped. He didn't dare put the woman on her horse. Frightened as she was, she'd probably race off and end up breaking her neck. He looped her mare's reins around his saddle horn.

"Wait!" she burst out. "I have m-money. I can p-pay you more."

"What are you clatterin' about? I don't want your money." Buck nearly added if he'd wanted to rob her, he'd have done it and been gone by now. "We got to find shelter before we freeze to death. You live nearby?"

The woman stared up at him, her eyes rounding. Was she so addled she couldn't understand what he was asking? Maybe the cold had gotten to her. He'd take her and head down that road, which he assumed led into Girard.

He lifted the woman onto Goliath and mounted behind her. There wasn't enough room in the saddle for two, especially with all those skirts, but somehow he managed to get her situated across his lap. Thank the saints she didn't go into conniptions.

The ends of her cloak snapped in the wind. She shuddered so hard it made *his* teeth rattle. He opened his greatcoat then wrapped them both in the blanket and oilskin.

She burrowed into his chest like a baby rabbit. Her vulnerability tugged at his heart. Wouldn't kill him to offer her comfort.

He curled his arm around her. "Warmer now?"

She nodded her head.

"Where do you live?"

"I...*we* have a farm...I'll see to it you're well compensated if you take me there."

So, she was married. No surprise. With so few women out here, even a crazy one would be snatched up, especially one smelling this sweet and with soft curves in all the right places.

"How far is it?"

"Up the road, just a little ways."

"A little ways? As in few minutes?"

"I...I'm not sure exactly."

Buck snorted in disbelief. She didn't know where she lived? "We can't wander around. It's getting dark."

"We could make Girard. It's maybe a half hour's ride."

Maybe? He turned the stallion and peered in the direction she'd indicated, gave a grumbling assent. He was going to Girard anyway. Although he wasn't sure they'd make it before night set in and the temperatures dropped even lower. "Anything else nearby?"

"Our farm..."

"That you can't find."

Shit.

Grudgingly, Buck nudged Goliath onto the road. According to his cousin's letter, thousands of settlers had poured into these former Indian lands. If so, where were they? Did they all live in town? Or was this strip of land reserved for the railroad's use? The exorbitant price they'd put on a godforsaken wilderness seemed ludicrous. Of course, why anyone would want to farm it was also a mystery. Didn't matter though. Sean had settled here, had worked the land, and now the railroad's owner—rich bastard—was trying to cheat him out of it.

Buck tilted his head down to keep the wind from snatching his hat. The woman turned her face into his vest like she was trying to warm her nose. He cradled her closer, felt her relax in his arms. Warmth spread through him, and not just from the heat of their bodies, it came from someplace deep inside, a part of him he'd thought was long dead.

He squelched a flare of alarm. Concern for another living creature, that's all it was. Nothing more. He didn't give a tinker's damn about anybody, save his family— what was left of it.

They'd gone only a few miles when something caught his eye. He straightened and peered at a shadow. Whatever it was, it was big. Then he sighed with relief. "There's a barn over there."

She peeked out from beneath her hood. "It's abandoned, and the house was burned down. We can't stop there."

The hell they couldn't. "So long as there's a roof, we're stopping."

The stranger wrestled the barn door open and then dragged Amy off his horse. Before she could protest, her feet left the ground and he carried her into the dark interior. He dumped her on a pile of hay before vanishing back into the night, taking his warmth with him.

The wind shrieked in a wild tantrum and the barn creaked and moaned, as the stranger rustled about getting the horses settled somewhere on the other side. Amy stared blindly into the darkness, hugging the blanket, shivering, both from cold and lingering fear.

Seemed her rescuer wasn't the mysterious assailant who'd been skulking around after her. When the towering stranger had come up on her out of nowhere, she'd feared the worst and had gone for her gun in the buggy. The first time, he'd pulled her away before she could find it. Then, once she'd retrieved her pistol, he'd disarmed her. That he'd done it so easily was beyond humiliating. The cold must've slowed her mind and her reflexes. Even after he assured her he meant no harm, she'd worried he might only be telling her that so he could take her somewhere and abuse her before killing her. But he hadn't done more than cuddle her close, as if he wished to comfort her. For some inexplicable reason, she'd let him.

She chewed her lip, her thoughts whirling. If the Land League hadn't sent this frighteningly large fellow after her, where had he come from? He didn't look like a farmer, not with that Henry repeater holstered by his saddle and those revolvers strapped to his hips. Not to mention the knife as long as her forearm, which she'd discovered while huddled close to him. On the other hand, he might've armed himself in light of the increased violence in these parts.

Was that why her typically protective suitor hadn't made it back to town to escort her? Had Fletcher been waylaid by thugs working for the Land League? Or had he, too, been caught unawares by the change in the weather? If she'd known a late winter storm was imminent, she would've found someplace to stay in town, despite the risk.

Her nerves jumped at the scrape of a match. Light flared. Amy blinked as the stranger approached with a lit taper. Not just well armed, but well prepared.

Her gaze traveled from his scuffed, square-toed boots up long legs encased in checkered gray trousers of the California style cowboys favored. A heavy greatcoat hung past his knees. Around his neck, he wore a faded bandana, its color indistinguishable. His hat looked older than his shoes and its brim shadowed his expression. Was he one of the countless drifters passing through, looking for work?

"At least we'll have some light." His spoke in a low drawl, raspy as gravel in a dry creek bed. Strangely enough, she found the sound soothing. After securing the candle to the underside of a bucket, he set it nearby. "Careful not to knock this over. I'd build a fire, but with all the hay this place would go up like a torch."

Why did he feel the need to explain as one would to a child or a very old person?

"My mental faculties aren't so deficient I'd set the

barn on fire." She tried to adjust the blanket more securely, but her numb fingers wouldn't obey and it kept slipping off.

The stranger knelt, removing his hat. Flaxen hair fell in tangled waves past his collar, and the light revealed a ruggedly handsome face—in sore need of a shave. Brown whiskers bristled on lean cheeks and a tawny mustache nearly hid his mouth. But it was his eyes that captured her, their color, so unusual—somewhere between blue and gray, but pale as a washed-out sky.

"Give me your hands." He stripped off his gloves as he issued the command. Rather than waiting to see whether she'd obey, he began to chafe them between his calloused palms. "How come you're not wearing gloves?"

She bristled at the disapproving tone. He'd made it clear he believed she was a simpleton.

"I had need of my fingernails." She didn't explain the problem with the frozen harness strap, which had necessitated the removal of her gloves to pick away the ice. No doubt she'd dropped them during their struggle, and she'd been too flustered to retrieve her muff. Not that he would've let her go back to the buggy after she'd pulled a gun on him.

His wintery eyes narrowed. Along his cheekbone, a crusted line of dried blood marked a scratch she'd put there. Her insides coiled tighter. She shouldn't have made it sound as if she'd intended to hurt him. She didn't even remember doing it. All she recalled was the sheer terror that had overcome her when he grabbed her.

He released her hands and began to unbutton his vest and shirt.

Her heart fluttered with renewed fear. "What...what are you doing?"

"Ravishing your frozen fingers."

Capturing her hands, he threaded them through the

opening in his shirt, then sandwiched her palms against his chest. His body radiated heat like a furnace, and soon her fingers began to burn. With a moan, she tried to pull away, but he held fast.

"It's good if you feel pain. That means you won't lose your fingers."

Lose her fingers? *God forbid.* She burrowed through crisp hair on his chest, seeking the warm skin beneath.

His eyes widened a split second before his features turned to stone.

The heat she'd taken from him went straight to her face. What was she *thinking* to touch him like that? She stilled her hands.

The muscles beneath her fingers flexed. Her skin tingled in response. The startling sensation spread up her arms and curled around the tips of her breasts. With a gasp, she yanked her hands away and tucked them under her arms.

Almighty. Was she *attracted* to him? She'd never been drawn to rough men like this one. It had to have something to do with the strangeness of the situation. She hugged the blanket as her teeth started chattering. He hadn't molested her, but that didn't mean he wouldn't if she kept touching him. Cold or not, she wasn't taking the chance.

He reached over and snatched away the blanket.

She squeaked in protest. "What are you doing?"

"We need to get you warmed up."

"If you t-take my blanket, how do you suggest I get warm?"

He grasped a handful of her damp cloak. "You won't, if you stay in those wet clothes."

He was right. Amy cursed another lapse in reason. Her fears had rendered her senseless. "I should've retrieved my valise. There is a dry outfit in there—"

"Fair to say it ain't dry any longer." He snagged his

saddlebag. Thrusting his hand inside, he withdrew several items of clothing. "Here, put these on."

She wrinkled her nose. He didn't really believe she'd don his undergarments, did he?

He frowned at her and shook them. *Yes, he did.* And she'd be a fool to refuse dry clothes. Perhaps his shirt over her underclothes, just until her other things dried out.

Before she could act, he plopped down, yanked her foot into his lap and began to undo the laces on her boot. His touch set off another bout of shivers that had nothing to do with the temperature of the air.

"What are you doing?" She jerked her foot out of his hands.

"Taking off your wet clothes, since you seem too addled to take care of it."

"I am *not* addled." She scooted back. "I can tend to myself, if you would be so kind as to give me some privacy."

He stood, seemingly tall as a mountain, his eyes gleaming like polished silver. "Good to see you recall how to get undressed. I wasn't looking forward to doing it for you."

Buck strode to where he'd stabled his horse, anxious to get away from the all-too-appealing woman he'd rescued. He'd held her close enough to feel those sweet curves. Come to find out, her face was just as nice. Still, he hadn't been prepared for the surge of lust when she'd splayed her fingers over his chest.

She'd felt something, too. He'd seen it in her eyes. And for a half second, he'd considered taking her right there on the hay. Only, she was frightened…and *crazy.* Couldn't forget that.

Inside the stall, he scooped up a handful of straw and began to dry the remaining dampness from the stallion's smoky coat. Goliath pawed and snorted, preening for the mare in the adjacent stall.

"You better behave," Buck whispered. "If she's like her owner, she'll kick you into next Sunday for messing with her."

The stallion whinnied.

"You're right. Might be worth it. Still, better not take the chance. Besides, that woman's none of my business." Buck's hand stilled. He'd made her his business when he brought her in out of the cold.

He sighed, shaking his head. They were stuck here for the night, so he had to make the best of it. But once he got her safely to wherever it was she was going, he'd find his cousin and focus on the only business he cared about—getting justice for his family.

From the other side of the stall came the unmistakable shush of garments being shed.

Buck wrestled his conscience, but the temptation was too strong. Taking advantage of his height, he peeked over the wall, curious as a crow with a shiny object in sight.

She had her back to him and he couldn't see a thing below her neck because she'd pushed up a pile of hay and was hiding behind it. *Smart gal...* and not as crazy as he first thought.

Her green dress went over a rail, along with countless petticoats, each fancier than its neighbor. Lastly, she set aside a bedraggled headpiece too small to call a hat, but with plumes he was sure were peacock feathers.

He shook his head, more intrigued than ever. With those fancy clothes, she could've walked right off a fashion plate in one of those ladies' magazines he'd seen in his stepfather's mercantile. Who was she, and what was she doing out here, smack dab in the middle of former Indian land? This place was still wild, and based on what Sean had reported, it was getting a lot wilder since the settlers' dispute with the railroad had exploded into an all-out war. Was her husband involved? That might explain why she'd reacted with fear.

Buck's heart raced as he watched her lift her arms to shake out a glorious length of chestnut hair. The candle's light reflected off golden strands. He swallowed hard, his hands fisting. God, he would kill to run his fingers through those tresses.

His mind conjured an image of the voluptuous beauty stark naked, beckoning him to join her on his blanket. Sizzling heat shot straight to his groin. Biting back a tortured groan, he turned away before she caught him peeking at her.

He rested his arms on Goliath's withers. "Just my luck. I had to rescue a *Venus*," he muttered. "Why couldn't she be ugly and buck-toothed?"

"Sir?" Her voice drifted over, breathy and uncertain. "If you want to come back, I'm decent."

Decent? Sure she was. But those curves weren't, and no shirt of his was going to help. He'd lied through his teeth when he told her he wasn't looking forward to unwrapping her. Except, she'd claw his eyes out before he could see anything.

He touched the scratch across his cheekbone and winced. Should've announced his intentions before grabbing her, but he'd been so shocked to see a woman out alone in this weather, then when that buggy started rocking, well, he'd just leapt off his horse and raced to the rescue. A wry smile twisted his lips. That gal sure hadn't seen a white knight. Not that he was interested in being one.

Against his better judgment, he ventured back to where he'd left her, sitting on the hay next to the bucket that held the candle. She had her legs tucked up beneath her and that scratchy blanket wrapped clear to her neck and was clutching at it like she was afraid he might take it away. His conscience tweaked him. He'd all but threatened to strip her if she didn't undress. It'd been too long since he'd been in the company of decent women. This would be an uncomfortable night for both of them if he didn't at least try to ease her fears.

He unbuckled his gun belt, wrapped it around the guns and went down on one knee, carefully laying the revolvers within her reach. The Bowie knife went beside the holsters. Her eyes followed his every move. At last, her shoulders lowered and the tense expression softened. More than that, he could actually *feel* her distress draining.

Buck rocked back on his heels, bemused. Over the years, he'd honed his instincts, relying on gut-level intuition to stay alive. But this strange connection seemed to extend to an ability to pick up on the ebb and flow of her emotions, which tugged like the current in a river.

She offered a slight smile. "Thank you for saving me, Mr.—?"

"O'Connor," he blurted, absurdly pleased by the gratitude shining in her eyes. On second thought, he should've given her an alias. Still, it was unlikely she'd ever heard of him. He wasn't as well known as his friend Cole Younger. "Couldn't let you turn into an icicle."

His breath clouded the air. Come to think of it, this ramshackle barn was damn frigid. It offered shelter from the sleet, but did little to keep the cold out. "Here, let me pile up some hay. It'll block the drafts and keep you warm."

"What about you? Are you warm enough?" She hugged the blanket, shivering.

"You want my coat?" His hands went to the buttons. Should've thought to offer it earlier.

Her eyes widened. "No, I wasn't implying that. I just thought *you* might be cold. We can share the hay."

For a moment, he was speechless. It'd been so long since anyone cared about his comfort, he hadn't expected it and didn't know how to respond. He shrugged to hide how much her concern touched him.

"Ah, don't worry about me. You hungry?" He rummaged through the saddlebag, finding the last piece of jerky. "It's not much, but it'll take the edge off."

"Thank you." She gifted him with a smile that snatched his breath.

He leaned back on one arm, trying his damnedest not to look like an infatuated schoolboy. Instead of sitting here mooning over her, he ought to find out what he could about the local situation. Whatever she knew might come in handy when he started searching for that railroad promoter.

"So, you live out here, Mrs., uh…"

"Langford," she finished.

He tried the name in his head. *Mrs. Langford.* Nope, he preferred Venus.

She bit off a small piece of jerky with perfect white teeth, chewed slowly and swallowed before continuing. "Yes, I live…" Her voice trailed off and her lashes lowered.

He leaned forward, worried. "Something wrong?"

She shook her head. "I'm sorry, Mr. O'Connor. I wasn't honest before. I don't live around here. I was headed for a friend's house before starting back to Fort Scott."

That she'd fibbed about where she lived didn't surprise him. She'd done it so he'd think her husband was nearby. But where she was going astonished him. "Fort Scott? That's another two days' ride."

"By rail it's only a couple hours. But the line hasn't

reached Girard yet, so we have to go a few miles north to meet the workers' train."

"We?"

"I was traveling with an escort. He attended a meeting earlier today in Baxter Springs and didn't make it back. We'd arranged to stay overnight at a friend's farm, so I thought I'd meet him there."

"Your husband *abandoned* you in Girard?"

Irritation flickered across her face. "He's not my husband, and he didn't abandon me."

It was on the tip of Buck's tongue to ask why she was traveling with a man who wasn't her husband. But then, what did he care who she traveled with? He opted for a safer question. "Why were you there? From what I hear, it's not exactly a safe place for a woman."

She finished chewing the last bite before responding. "I had business in town."

"Business?"

Her lips sealed. Apparently, she didn't wish to elaborate.

Buck smoothed his mustache with his thumb and forefinger, mulling over her hesitation. Just what kind of business would a wealthy lady have with a bunch of rowdy settlers? When he'd come up on her, she'd been terrified, even after he told her he was trying to help. Had even offered him money. *More* money…

His scalp began to tingle, a sure sign something wasn't right. He leaned forward, draping an arm over his knee to appear casual. "I didn't mean to frighten you when I rode up. You must've been expecting trouble."

"Trouble is one way to put it…." She toyed with a curl at her cheek, not meeting his eyes. "You see, I thought you were going to kill me."

Get the rest of the book now from Amazon.

Other Books by the Author

In the *Steam! Romance and Rails Series*

PASSION'S PRIZE
(with Jennifer Jakes and Jacqui Nelson)

KATE'S OUTLAW
(a novella included in Passion's Prize)

HER BODYGUARD

A DANGEROUS PASSION

FUGITIVE HEARTS

www.eeburke.com

To learn about upcoming and new releases, please join
my newsletter:
https://www.eeburke.com/news.html

E.E. Burke writes romance from the heart, woven with history the way it really happened in the old American West. Her latest series, *Steam! Romance and Rails*, includes *Passion's Prize*, *Her Bodyguard* and *A Dangerous Passion*. Her writing has earned accolades in regional and national contests, including the prestigious Golden Heart®.

Over the years, she's been a disc jockey, a journalist and an advertising executive, before finally getting around to pursuing her dream of writing novels. The stories she writes are as deeply rooted in American soil as her family, which she can trace back to the earliest colonists and through both sides of the Mason-Dixon line. She lives in Kansas City with her husband and three daughters, the greatest inspiration of all.